I0667099

The Lost Stories of SHERLOCK HOLMES 2nd Edition

by John H Watson, M.D.

edited by Tony Reynolds
illustrated by Chris Coady

Paperback ISBN 9781780923512
ePub ISBN 9781780923529
PDF ISBN 9781780923536

Published in the UK by MX Publishing
335 Princess Park Manor, Royal Drive, London, N11 3GX
www.mxpublishing.co.uk

Cover design by www.staunch.com

TO
CHRISTOPHER
who wanted to hear about the Giant Rat.

CONTENTS

EDITOR'S FOREWORD

On the death of my grandmother, Emma Mary Reynolds (*née* Watson) of Netherfield in Sussex, my father came into possession of three deed-boxes. He asked me to look through them and – after forcing the locks, as the keys had been lost long before – I found that they contained the papers of John H. Watson, M.D., famous as the companion and biographer of Sherlock Holmes.

The papers are of very various kinds, but among those which are of more than family interest are records of many cases in which Dr. Watson assisted Sherlock Holmes. The bulk of these are merely notes which for whatever reason he did not work up into a narrative but there is also a number of stories which were completed but not published.

I believe that some of these stories remained unpublished because on reflection Dr. Watson did not think them interesting enough for the general reader. In most cases however, it is clear from the text that they were withheld for a reason: this was usually to respect the privacy of Holmes' clients, but sometimes for other ends such as to conceal facts from the authorities or to meet the demands of state security.

As all the parties involved are long dead I am of the opinion that these reasons are no longer cogent and I have selected nine of the adventures to make up this volume. I hope these will serve to cast more light on the methods and genius of the great detective and on the assistance he received from his steadfast friend; my forebear, Dr. John Watson.

Tony Reynolds

THE GIANT RAT OF SUMATRA

Y friend Sherlock Holmes remains adamant that the world is not yet ready for the story of the clipper *Matilda Briggs* and that fearsome beast, the giant rat of Sumatra. He has however allowed me to commit it to paper, and has refreshed my memory on many of the details. I have no doubt, seeing the pace at which Science has altered all our lives in these last decades of the nineteenth century, that the time will soon come when the matters described herein will be fully understood and our savants will be able to deal with the dangers embodied in the facts I have to relate.

I recall that it was a chilly November's evening when Sherlock Holmes and I were seated before a fire at 221B Baker Street, sipping a little port and reminiscing on our past adventures.

"The days grow longer for me Watson, while in truth they grow shorter," complained my friend. "There have been few cases in the last six months to try my powers to any extent. Even your noted powers of sensationalism have failed to make much of such poor material. I can feel the fog and damp rusting my brain as I sit here idly."

"Come now, Holmes," I said, as bluffly as I could, wary of the black depression that so often gripped him when he was unable to use his remarkable talents, and in which he was likely to seek false solace in his little vials of cocaine. "A few weeks of rest can only do you good. Why not think of it as an opportunity to work on your reagents to distinguish bloodstains? Did you not say that Harvey's latest research proves that –"

I broke off because at that moment there came the pounding of a heavy man running up the stairs, followed at some distance by the indignant protests of Mrs. Hudson.

"Ah, Watson," said my friend, sitting up abruptly in his chair, "perhaps we can hope that this worthy mariner brings

1

us a problem that will challenge us. Certainly he thinks it urgent enough."

"Mariner?"

"Come, Watson, the rhythm of his feet as he ascends the stairs bespeaks the roll of the sea. He is also certainly of the merchant service – Come in!" he called as a loud knocking came at the door, "– for we must expect more calm and discipline from those who face Her Majesty's enemies in our glorious Navy."

By this time indeed the sailor stood before us. He was a man of mature years, his face brown and wrinkled, especially around the eyes, where years of watching a distant horizon had left their mark. He was in uniform, the blue faded from long wear, but clean and pressed. He wore, I noted, the epaulettes that denoted that he held the rank of mate.

"Mr. Holmes?" he said, looking from one to the other of us. "I must speak to Mr. Holmes at once."

"I am he," said Holmes. "Please pull up a chair and tell us of your difficulties. Thank you Mrs. Hudson," he said, as that lady arrived red-faced and puffing at our door, "I'm very sorry you have been inconvenienced, but my client here has a most urgent problem. Nothing less than murder, surely," he added, turning again to the sailor, "would cause a man of your rank to come in person, and in such haste."

Mrs. Hudson bobbed her head in acknowledgement and retired, obviously put out at having her house used so cavalierly.

"Two murders, Mr. Holmes," said the sailor grimly, as he seated himself on one of our dining chairs, "and cannibalism into the bargain."

"Dear me, this is very distressing," said Holmes, managing manfully to conceal his delight. "Pray tell us all the facts, beginning if you please well before the incidents you speak of."

"I will, sir. My name is Peter Bowman, and I am the first mate of the *Matilda Briggs* of Brixham. We sailed a month ago from the island of Sumatra with a cargo of mahogany and copra. The captain, Mr. Blake, is also the owner of the vessel and we ply to and from the China Seas, carrying whatever cargo is profitable.

"On this occasion, the first evening we docked at the port of Panang on Sumatra, a Chinaman, Mr. Lee, came aboard. Captain Blake was expecting him, although he'd said nothing to me, and they spent a couple of hours together in his cabin. The next night the captain gave us all shore leave and said he'd stand the watch himself. When we got back early in the morning, I was told that Mr. Lee was shipping some cargo with us and would be sailing with us to London."

"Is the captain always so considerate of his crew's welfare that he allows them to carouse in the taverns while he himself guards the ship?" asked Sherlock Holmes languidly.

"Indeed he was not, sir. He was a hard man, Captain Blake was, and believed in discipline."

"You say 'was'. I take it he was one of the unfortunate victims?"

"Yes sir, that was later when we were near the Cape –"

"No, please, Mr. Bowman, I should not have interrupted you. Please continue your story from where you left off. Mr. Lee shipped some cargo you say. Can you tell us what it was?"

"Not exactly, sir, no. It was already aboard when I got back from shore leave. It was about twenty barrels of something heavy, and when I asked the captain what was in them he said they were some sort of ore. I didn't ask any more: the captain was always careful to mind his own business. And Mr. Lee hardly said a word to anyone."

"Quite. A characteristic of the Chinese race. Please go on with your account."

"It wasn't a happy voyage back, sir. Not that anything particular went wrong, you understand, but we were all uneasy, what with having the Chinaman on board and hanging around all the time. And none of us liked to go into the cargo hold. Not that we needed to much, of course, but it seemed very close down there, and we didn't like it.

"We were about three weeks into the voyage and just about to round the Cape when the captain died. It was a rough night, rougher than we'd had so far. I had the deck watch and I was worried that the timber we carried might shift. The captain was in the wheelhouse. He usually took the wheel in rough weather. Didn't rightly trust anybody else with his ship, I suppose. Well, I took a lantern and checked below. Everything seemed secure, so I went forward to my station. Suddenly, we went broadside to the waves. I was almost thrown overboard, where I wouldn't have lasted long in those seas. There was a yelling and shouting as the hands came on deck, and one of them, the bo'sun, Peters, got to the wheel and brought us back on course.

"I got to the wheelhouse as soon as I could; the hands were standing at the rail outside, groaning most of them in fear and horror. I didn't bother with them but went straight inside and found the captain dead on the floor, in a pool of blood. The back of his neck was covered with blood, I took off my kerchief and wiped away as much of it as I could. He seemed to have been stabbed right through the nape of his neck. A strange blow, sir, but effective. It must have cut his spine and killed him at once. I rolled him over, and then – oh Mr. Holmes, I've been at sea all my life and seen many grim sights, but nothing to match this. His left cheek seemed to have been cut and chewn away! Behind it was nothing but the red jaw and the white teeth grinning up at me."

He halted at this point and stared at the floor, breathing heavily. Holmes started to his feet. "Mr. Bowman, in our anxiety to hear your story, we have forgotten our hospitality. Let me offer you a glass of whisky." He poured a large glass as he spoke and handed it to the sailor, who tossed back half of it at a gulp. "Now, if it does not distress you, I must ask what exactly do you mean by 'cut and chewn'?"

"Just that, Mr. Holmes. The flesh seemed partly to have been slashed away by a sharp knife, and partly to be crushed and torn as meat is when a dog mauls it."

"I understand. You buried the body at sea, no doubt?"

"We did, sir; the next morning. So far from port and at those latitudes we had no choice."

"Of course, although that has unfortunately robbed me of valuable data. Were there any signs of a struggle or any other significant indications at the scene?"

"No, Mr. Holmes, although you must remember that a high sea was running, and the deck was constantly awash."

"Also unfortunate, but please continue."

"As the senior officer I took charge of the ship. I immediately questioned every member of crew as to where they were at the time and what they had heard. I got nothing from this. Most of them were in the fo'csle, a few were in their hammocks or below decks generally. No-one had heard anything."

"Was there anyone you questioned with, shall we say, especial care?"

"There was. The captain as I said was a hard man and several of the crew had cause to dislike him. The master-at-arms, Bailey, had had arguments with him. They were both hot-tempered men, and although the captain said nothing straight, we all knew Bailey would be paid off at the end of the voyage. Still, I can't believe Bailey would mutilate a man like the captain was, however hot he became. A couple of the Lascars too, I questioned pretty hard. The captain didn't like blacks; he was always saying they were shiftless and he only signed them on because they were dirt cheap. He took his boot to them pretty regular, and it would be like them to knife a man in the dark from behind; and it's only a generation since most of them took it for granted you ate your enemy after you'd killed him. And then of course there was Mr. Lee."

"Ah yes, the mysterious Mr. Lee. What was his account?"

5

"Simply that he was in his cabin asleep. He had heard nothing and seen nothing. Still, it was a good ten minutes after the ship yawed that he appeared on deck. What was he doing all that time? He didn't look half-asleep either. I don't know: with Chinamen you can't tell what they're thinking, and they'll never tell you. But I've been to those Eastern parts for a long time, Mr. Holmes, and I know how quick they are with their knives, and I know something of the nasty tricks they get up to in the name of their heathen gods."

"I would have hoped at least for some bruising or grazing on the skin of the assailant, or almost certainly, blood on his clothing or in his hair."

"There was none, sir, that I could see."

"How did you proceed?"

"I didn't have enough cause to put anyone in irons. All I could do was write it all down in the log, and issue orders that all deck duties after dark were to be done in pairs. The next day we hove-to and I read the service over the captain and sent him over the side wrapped in sailcloth. We had another ten day's sailing to London, and we all had to work harder because of the doubled watches, but no-one complained. Nothing more happened, although we were all looking over our shoulders, I can tell you.

"We docked at the Royal Docks early this morning, and I was very busy arranging for unloading and storage of the cargo and in sending a telegram to captain Blake's brother telling him of the accident and asking him to come and sort out the new ownership. I'm not much with words, sir, and it took a lot of crossings out before I came up with something I felt able to send off to him. Then early tonight, we had our second killing.

"It was about seven o'clock – well dark of course at this time of year and in this weather. I was in the captain's cabin trying to make head or tail of the paperwork, when I heard a scream. I dashed out into the companionway and it came again. It seemed to be from 'tweendecks, where the crew

6

hang their hammocks. I got there in a couple of minutes, maybe, but it was all over. It was Bailey, the master-at-arms. He was still in his hammock, Mr. Holmes, but it was wrapped around him, trussing him up as neat as neat. And from his body great drips of blood were still falling and splashing on the lower deck.

"We untangled him, but it was all over. There were four parallel slashes of a knife across his chest, not very deep, perhaps done with quick back-and-forth passes of a double-edged blade. They weren't enough to kill him. What did kill him was a great tear in his stomach. We could see his guts spilling out through the rip. A very nasty death, Mr. Holmes."

"Indeed," said Holmes abstractedly. "Tell me Mr. Bowman, when would the unloading of the cargo have commenced?"

This question seemed so unconnected to the facts under consideration that both I and the sailor stared at Holmes for a few seconds. At last Bowman replied.

"It would have been about an hour after dawn this coming morning Mr. Holmes. The chief stevedore hires his men at dawn and gives them their orders."

"I see. Please go on."

"There is little more to tell. We called the police at once, and men from Scotland Yard are on the ship now. As for me, as soon as I had told the inspector what I knew, I took a cab for Baker Street. I don't believe the police can find who killed my shipmates, Mr. Holmes, but maybe you can."

"I cannot thank you enough for having brought me this problem, Mr. Bowman. Is your cab waiting?"

"It is."

"Then scnd it away: we will get a four-wheeler and make all speed to the docks. Come, Watson: the game is afoot!"

The cab rattled along the cobbles of the Strand, then windingly through the City, then through mean streets to the Docks. It was a long journey, mostly passed in silence as my friend did not care to talk. We saw few people, and those looked as if they would rather not be abroad on that swart and foggy evening.

At the Royal Docks the scene changed. We would have found the moorings of the *Matilda Briggs* without assistance by the crowd of sightseers that had gathered. These were being kept well back from the gangplank by a large and bewhiskered constable. Our cab approached, and the policeman pushed a suspicious face inside.

"Good evening, gentlemen," he said, "I must ask your business here."

"I am Sherlock Holmes," said my friend politely, "I would like to speak to the inspector on duty."

The constable saluted. "Good evening sir. Inspector Lestrade is in charge of the case. I've no doubt he will be pleased to speak to you. The constable on board will direct you."

We walked up the gangplank and introduced ourselves again to the policeman on duty at the head of it. He accompanied us to the captain's cabin, beat a sharp tattoo on the door and opened it at once. "Mr. Sherlock Holmes and Dr. Watson to see you, Inspector," he announced.

The cabin was not overlarge, and already contained Lestrade, seated at a desk, and a gentleman of Chinese appearance who stood before him. Behind the Chinaman loomed a burly policeman. We three crowded in with some difficulty.

"Ah, Holmes," Lestrade greeted us genially, sinking deeper into his chair, "delighted to see you here. And you too Doctor. I'm afraid, however, that you won't find anything of interest here. An open and shut case I'm afraid; even we simple policemen were able to clear it up without your expert assistance."

"I was never in doubt that you would make a speedy arrest, Inspector," said Holmes affably. "Can I take it that Mr. Lee here is your prisoner?"

"Precisely. As a first routine precaution we obtained a magistrate's warrant and searched the baggage of everyone on board. The sailors had only their sea-chests, but Mr. Lee here had a very interesting assortment of gear." He indicated with his hand a strange miscellany on the desk. "That bottle appears to contain a powerful sleeping draught – we'll have it analysed of course – those leather straps and buckles would hold a mad bull; that running noose has obvious uses in strangulation and that fishing trident has traces of blood on the tips. The curved knife we found up his sleeve: I've no doubt that was the murder weapon."

"An impressive haul, Inspector, I congratulate you. This does indeed greatly clarify the case," said Holmes.

"Clarify? It clears it up completely."

"There are perhaps one or two minor loose ends. Why for instance did Mr. Lee bring such a murderous collection abroad: did he always intend to wreak mayhem? And why so many instruments: surely they are over-complicated for the purpose? Would you care to enlighten us, Mr. Lee?"

The Chinaman said nothing, but merely stared impassively at Holmes.

"You can never get them to talk," said Lestrade dismissively, "But that doesn't matter. Let me get him in front of an English jury and show them that lot and he'll swing for sure, confession or no confession."

"No doubt," said my friend, "but with your permission, Inspector, I wonder if I might inspect the cargo hold?"

"You can if you want, Holmes, but we've taken a look, and there's nothing down there but a lot of wood."

"Thank you, Inspector. If I might explain my reasons, it seems to be that there is always the possibility of a stowaway, and the cargo hold is the only place on a small ship where he could possibly conceal himself."

Lestrade laughed incredulously. "This is fantastic even for you. You surely can't imagine that a man could conceal himself for a month and not leave traces. What would he eat, for instance?"

"Nevertheless, with your permission I will look."

9

Lestrade shrugged. "If you want, Holmes. We'll all come along: there's nothing more for me to do now, so I might as well stretch my legs."

We proceeded on to the deck and then along to a large hatch, which Mr. Bowman raised for us. He descended first and lit a couple of lanterns which were stored below the steps. Holmes and I went next, then Lestrade, then Mr. Lee and his escort. Below decks it was stuffy and smelt, although not unpleasantly, of timber and the sickly scent of copra.

"A useful cargo," commented Holmes. "Mahogany to enhance the dwellings that are being built at such a pace in our city, and the flesh of the coconut to form the base of the many soaps and lotions that hygiene requires."

Without further words he took out his magnifying glass and holding that in one hand and one of the lanterns in the other began to scuttle about the hold, clambering over the baulks of timber and occasionally burrowing into the bales of copra. At first he ranged widely, then his efforts became more frenetic and more localised. At last he actually dived into the pile of timber and let out a shout of triumph.

"Come and look at this, inspector!"

We hurried across to where Holmes had now extricated himself. He stood almost at the stern, where the ends of the great timbers were visible. They had been roughly squared off with an adze or some such primitive instrument and laid along the length of the ship. Many of them were venerable forest giants, fully five feet across at the widest point of their boles. Their natural variation meant that the timber could not be close packed and there were many gaps in the pile. Holmes indicated one of the largest of these, perhaps two feet square.

Lestrade took the lantern from his constable and bent down suspiciously. "Faugh, what a smell of rats!" he said.

"Please inspector, go further in," urged Holmes.

Reluctantly Lestrade did as requested, and wriggled on his stomach further into the wood. "Why," came his voice, "there's been a regular nest of them! There's straw and droppings all over the place."

"Not a nest, I believe, inspector. The indications are that there was only one beast."

"Why should anyone want to keep a rat down here? What good is a rat to anyone, anyway?" replied Lestrade, climbing out of the hole with some effort.

"Look at the size of the droppings, Inspector, and the length of its claw marks on the wood. I would estimate that the rat is no less than four feet long! That is why it had to be kept in secret."

"But that's preposterous!" exclaimed Lestrade, as I and Bowman expressed similar incredulity.

"Nevertheless, that is its size," said Holmes, "the markings leave no doubt. This construction here," he said, stirring with his foot a clumsy wooden lattice, joined by large clenched nails, "sealed the animal into its quarters. There is also no doubt that it was being cared for by Mr. Lee. I have found strands of red silk, which appear to match the robe he now wears, caught on the rough edges of the timber. There is also a trail of bits of copra leading to this den." He turned to Mr. Lee. "At night you went below, using the small cargo hatch near your cabin. You fed the rat from one of the bales of copra and saw to such of its needs as you could. Fortunately for you, they have a great tenacity for life, so a few weeks in the dark would not do the beast any great harm. You wished to bring it alive to England. For what purpose, may I ask?"

Lee continued to stand in sullen silence.

"Come, come, Mr. Lee," said Holmes suavely. "Do you not realise what this means? It is clear that it was the rat that carried out the killings, and consequently, although there are still charges that might be brought against you, your life at least is not forfeit. It is entirely in your own interests to give us more details."

"Very well," said Lee, speaking at last. "I bring rat. I take him to British Museum and sell him. Your scientists very

11

interested in this rat. Captain Blake know all about him and agree."

"Ah, the unfortunate Captain Blake. How did the rat get free on that occasion?"

"There was great storm. I stumble when I give rat food. It rush past me on to deck. When I get to Captain it too late. I put rope on rat while it feeding and prick it until it leave him."

"Hence the blood on the trident. It will be possible to establish that it belongs to a rodent rather than a man," said Holmes. "And this evening's incident of course occurred because you had to move the rat. To leave it longer would have meant discovery by the dockers; and you no longer had the assistance of Captain Blake to clear the ship."

Lee bowed. "Yes. I try to give rat sleeping stuff, but it very angry, very powerful. It spring at me and knock me down. I think it kill me, but I beat it off with cage door. Then it run away: kill first man it find."

Holmes nodded. "One can only imagine the fury and exuberance of the beast in finding itself free after so many weeks. Perhaps it hurled itself at Bailey to gain revenge on mankind for its confinement. And now, Mr. Lee, where is the rat?"

Lee shook his head. "Rat gone. I not know where."

"And there you have it, Inspector," said Holmes. "A vicious killer is on the loose in the East End. We must spare no efforts to capture it."

Lestrade looked disgusted. Far from finding himself hailed as the staunch agent of the law who had apprehended his man within an hour of receiving his orders, he had to undertake a difficult and doubtful campaign against an elusive adversary.

"I had better get back to Scotland Yard and have a word with my superiors," he said gruffly. "As for you, my man," he continued, turning to Lee, "we'll let you go for now, but you're to stay on board, and we'll be back soon with a lot more questions, see?"

Lee bowed in acquiescence.

"We also must be away," said Holmes. "Come Watson, back to Baker Street. It may be that we will be able to render further assistance to the inspector in this matter."

I found the next few days difficult to endure. I am not happy sitting for long periods without action. As for Holmes, he obtained a large ordnance map of the East End and pinned it to the wall. With the help of a series of engineering drawings which arrived in a constant stream from the great utility companies and engineering firms, he drew a network of lines in various colours over the map.

"Is it not obvious, Watson?" he said in reply to my enquiry. "Where does any rat hide? In the drains and sewers under the streets, of course. The fact that our rat is so much larger than its brethren does not mean that it does not share all their instincts. So I am preparing a plan of the possible hiding places. The different colours represent different sizes and depths of pipes, while the symbols represent the different sorts of access to those pipes. With this we map out the rat's domain."

"This is wonderful, Holmes," I said in admiration. "I must confess I never dreamed there was such complexity beneath our feet."

"How could it be otherwise, Watson? The rivers that used to run down to the Thames: the Fleet, the Holborn, the Tyburn and many others, are now all caged within brick walls by the hand of man, and the great city built above them so that now we only remember an echo of them in the names of our streets. Between them run the immense network of the companies' water and the cloaca that serve the teeming millions of the metropolis."

From time to time we would receive a policeman with a note from Lestrade, detailing the sightings of the great rat. Within a day of its escape it was the terror of the East End. Mothers locked up their children, women ventured on the streets only in the hours of daylight – short enough at that period – and even hardened drunkards would hesitate before joining the convivial company at the gin houses. Reports reached us of dogs and cats found eviscerated and half eaten. Fortunately, it became obvious that it preferred smaller prey to larger, and generally preferred to scavenge rather than to kill. Several denizens of the area spoke of having approached a pile of the rubbish that so often disfigures those streets, seeing it heave up and the giant rat climb forth and scuttle into the darkness. Whenever we were told of any such incident, Holmes marked a red spot on his map with a note of the date and time.

"You will appreciate, Watson, that a brute beast is in many ways easier to trap than a man. Certainly he has the advantages of great speed and access to tunnels where we cannot or dare not follow, but he does not have a man's ability to reason and to dissemble. He thinks only of the comfort of his lair, his need for food and a mate. He is a creature of habit, and once we know those habits, and provided we do not disturb them, we can capture the beast almost at our will. My net closes; it can now only be a matter of time before I have located its nest."

It was in fact the next day, that having had a flurry of messages detailing the rat's activities in the night, that Holmes gave an exclamation of triumph. "We have it, Watson! Here, in this conduit, it lurks awaiting the coming of darkness." With the end of his ruler, he pointed to a blue line on the map. "It is an overflow drain, taking excess flood water direct from Limehouse to the Thames. It is clear from the pattern of sightings that the beast has been roaming the area, looking for a suitable lair, and now has found what he considers to be ideal: a dry and remote spot with access to the streets where he can forage. Now, Watson, I must leave you for a few hours. We will meet again tonight, when I will value your support and the protection of your service revolver!"

The coming of dusk found us in Dangerfield Street in Limehouse. Holmes led me to a wide slot set into the edge of the road. A slight draught and a foetid odour came from it.

"Here, Watson, as I guess, the rat will make its foray. There are two other possibilities, and it may be that our watch will be in vain tonight; but let us make the attempt!"

He put his hand into a canvas bag he carried and pulled out a handful of grain.

"We will scatter some wheat at a little distance, in the hope that it will give the beast a line. We must do it on the same principle that fishermen lay ground-bait: enough to awaken the creature's appetite, but not enough to satisfy it."

He walked a few yards further to the mouth of a mean alley and again put down a small pile of wheat. "We have done what we can, Watson, let us now go to the place I have prepared," he announced. Walking a few yards into the alley, he knocked on a door. After a short time, an old man opened it, letting out a whiff of rotted matting and damp whitewash. He motioned us in. Holmes thanked him and led the way up the narrow stairs. At the top we turned into a small room overlooking the alley we had left.

"Here we will wait," said my friend. "I will take the first sentry duty if you will take the next. We are observing the shed yonder. In it I have placed some nicely half-rotted lamb that I obtained with little difficulty, I regret to say, from Smithfield. You will observe the door is ajar. I have changed the hinges for the rising butt type, in which the door automatically swings shut under its own weight. A length of black cotton from the meat holds the door open; if the thread should snap, the door will shut and latch. The system is therefore automatic, but we must not rely on it holding for any length of time. A rodent of such strength will surely break or gnaw its way through such a flimsy structure in a short time."

With few more words he took his station at the window. After an hour, when he felt his concentration was dropping, we changed places. It came to about eleven o'clock, when I was on watch for the fourth time, that I thought I saw a furtive movement in the gloom; I looked again and saw nothing, then suddenly heard the shed door clap shut.

Immediately afterwards there came a thud as if of some heavy weight thrown against the wood, then a furious loud scratching as of long claws.

"Quick, Watson!" shouted my friend. We leaped down the stairs, out the door and across the alley to the shed in less time than it takes to tell. There I saw to my horror that one of the planks was already splintering outwards under repeated blows.

"Take this!" shouted Holmes, grabbing up what I saw to be a fishing net and tossing one end to me. I had barely got a grip, when he put one hand on the latch and cried, "Now, stand firm!" and threw open the door.

As soon as the night sky penetrated the interior of the shed, I heard a scrabbling as the creature wheeled around and dashed out of the door. The shock as it struck the meshes of our net threw me off my feet, but I kept my hold and pulled back as hard as I could. Holmes ran athwart my path and wrapped the net securely around the animal.

"Now we have it!" said my companion, "I am as ever in your debt for your invaluable assistance. A unique and fascinating specimen!" He looked with delight at the rat, which was now hopelessly enmeshed, but still struggling furiously. For my part I stared in horror. The brute was fully four feet long, and dark grey in colour; its eyes caught mine and I think I have never seen such mindless hatred as they expressed. Its large yellow incisor teeth were bared, and its long claws protruded through the net as they strove impotently to rend our flesh.

"One last effort, Watson, and we can rest," said Holmes. He retired into the shed and returned at once dragging a large and stout cage. "I had this made up by a local carpenter today," he informed me. "The great thing about the East End is that the craftsmen are immediately to hand. It would have taken me much longer to arrange from Baker Street."

'I KEPT MY HOLD AND PULLED BACK AS HARD AS I COULD'

Under his direction, I took a length of slack net at one side of the animal, while he took another. With a good lift and swing the animal was penned. It was with relief that I saw Holmes chain the cage securely shut.

"If you will stand guard," said my friend, still in high spirits, "I will stroll over to a carter's I observed a few streets away. It is of course almost midnight, but a few sovereigns will doubtless compensate for a lost night's sleep."

It was half an hour later that Holmes returned with the cart. By that time the beast had become quiescent. I had also found a good-sized piece of sacking with which I covered the cage. The less people saw of the rat, the better, I considered. Holmes and I lifted the cage on to the vehicle, and then took our seats next to the driver.

"The Royal Docks, my good man!" announced Holmes, as the carter flicked his whip to set the horse into motion.

"The Docks!" I hissed to Holmes, "surely we should take the beast to Inspector Lestrade?"

"Have you no sense of property, Watson?" inquired my friend sardonically. "This animal belongs rightfully to Mr. Lee and it is our duty to return it to its owner."

I said no more, and it was less than an hour later that we found ourselves again at the moorings of the *Matilda Briggs*. After we had removed the cage, Holmes paid the driver, who gave us a word of thanks and turned his cart for home and bed.

As we started for the gangplank, the sinister form of Mr. Lee appeared on deck. I wondered if he ever slept. He bowed wordlessly to both of us.

"A very good morning to you, Mr. Lee!" said Holmes heartily from where he stood on the quay. "I have great pleasure in informing you that we have found your rat, and it reposes safe and well within this cage."

At this, Lee descended the gangplank with full Oriental dignity and walked over to the cage. He lifted a corner of the sacking and looked for a long moment at the beast. He stood

18

and replaced his hands in his sleeve, then bowed low, his whole attitude exuding suspicion.

"I very grateful to you gentlemen," he said, speaking his first words to us that night. "Rat very valuable to me. You will perhaps honour me by accepting a small gift?"

"Thank you indeed, Mr. Lee, but we could take nothing. We acted as our duty as citizens dictates, and of course for the thrill of the chase! Good evening, sir! Come, Watson."

We left, and my last view of Mr. Lee was of him standing motionless by the cage, staring after us.

As we sat in a cab on our way back to Baker Street I ventured to speak to Holmes. "No doubt the British Museum will buy the rat, but I would have thought that a circus would have paid more."

"You surely did not believe that flimsy story, Watson? The Natural History department of the British Museum would no doubt be interested, but they prefer their animals dead and stuffed. The Zoo would have been a better nomination, but I doubt Mr. Lee is familiar with our English institutions. No, Lee went to great trouble and danger to bring the rat to our shores alive; he must have anticipated a large profit. Captain Blake was also clearly involved with the scheme, and he also must have expected to be well paid. There is a person behind all this, Watson, a person who wanted the giant rat to be brought to him alive and in secret and who is able to pay for the privilege."

"Good heavens! Could it be some unholy criminal conspiracy?"

"It is possible, although there are indications in other directions. We will know for certain this coming night."

"You believe Lee will move so soon?"

"Why should he delay? The rat is a dangerous beast as we have seen, and no doubt he fears Lestrade will bring some charge against him for allowing the rat to escape. He will want to collect his money and leave the country as soon as possible."

So it was that the next night saw us again at the Royal Docks, this time at some distance on a corner of approach road where we could watch for activity at the *Matilda Briggs*, but would not ourselves be readily visible from her. We had slept until noon that day, so we both felt reasonably fresh.

It was at eight o'clock that a carter manoeuvred his conveyance to the ship. We watched as he and some sailors first loaded the cage containing the giant rat, then returned and began rolling down the gangplank the first of a succession of large barrels.

"My word, Holmes," said I, "I had forgotten the barrels! What could they possibly contain, do you think?"

"They contain pitchblende, Watson," said my friend. "Also known as uranite. When we were aboard the ship, I managed to pry a sample from one barrel in which a stave had loosened."

"Pitchblende? What are its uses?"

"Certain substances can be extracted from it, but it has no unique properties that I know of. We must hope that more information will make the matter clearer."

The sailors worked quickly and well. Shortly the cart was loaded and Mr. Lee took his place beside the driver, and they set off.

"We will follow on foot," said Holmes, "the speed of a cart is so sedate as to make pursuit in a cab conspicuous."

The chase was a weary one; long and slow. The cart went steadily westwards and after about three hours arrived at Oxford Street. From there it turned into Cavendish Square then into Harley Street. A short way up this august thoroughfare it came to a halt in front of an imposing town house.

"This is within your purview, doctor," said my friend, "whose house is this?"

"Why, I believe these are Dr. Trelawney's premises," I said. "I have heard him lecture on several occasions. His speciality is the science of nutrition. He is greatly in demand by the quality to advise them on their diet when they feel out of sorts, and he also gives a good deal of his time free to the Westminster Children's Hospital where he treats sickly infants."

"A worthy man," said Holmes. "Let us wait here a while."

Lee pulled at the bell, and a well-built man opened the door. I recognised Dr. Trelawney himself. Between the three men, the cargo was unloaded; there being long pauses after each item was carried into the house, as if it was being taken some distance. At last the job was done. The carter returned to his seat. Lee bowed low to the doctor, then turned and climbed up beside the driver. Trelawney raised his hand in farewell and re-entered his house.

"What shall we do now, Holmes?" I asked as the cart disappeared to the North.

"We shall question the good doctor," said my friend. "Why not? He has committed no crime."

With that, he walked to Dr. Trelawney's door and rang the bell himself. After a short time Trelawney appeared, looking suspicious.

"Good evening, sirs," he said shortly. "You are aware no doubt that it is almost midnight? I trust your business is urgent."

"I cannot in honesty say that," confessed Holmes, "but it was my efforts and those of Dr. Watson's here that recaptured the large rodent you have taken delivery of, and we have a natural, if I am afraid, impertinent, curiosity as to its subsequent fate."

"And your name, sir?"

"I am Sherlock Holmes."

"I have heard of you, Mr. Holmes. I must say that I regard the bulk of your activities as superfluous, given that we have had a disciplined police force for over half a century. However, I am grateful on this occasion for your intervention. I have been following the situation in the papers, and I feared that the rat would be killed, or even disappear for good, in which case my researches would be seriously delayed. Please step inside.

"Now, gentlemen," he said, when we all stood in the hall. "I have no particular objection to satisfying your curiosity: I intend in any case to give the fruits of my research to the world when it is complete. However, you must understand that I tell you everything in complete confidence. The results that will spring from my work will revolutionise society, and I fear the premature upheaval that may transpire if any hint of those developments should become known."

"In my profession as consulting detective, discretion is universally expected," said Holmes. "Your confidences are completely safe with me."

"And of course with me," I added.

"Very well sirs: please come with me."

Trelawney led the way to the third floor. There he unlocked a heavy door, using two keys: one for a lock set high on the door at about the level of his chin, and another for a lock set at knee height. We stepped inside to see a large room set up as a laboratory. At first glance it appeared normal: cages for experimental animals occupied one of the short walls; there were shelves of chemicals and reagents; a most comprehensive set of laboratory glassware was set out along a bench, and the general air was of that of a laboratory in any of our great teaching hospitals. The cage containing the giant rat was on the floor. As we entered the rat stared at us, and bared its teeth with indescribable menace. Perhaps I am fanciful, but I thought it recognised those who had deprived it of its liberty.

The only unusual feature at first glance was a table in the centre of the room bearing a large plaster relief model of what I recognised to be the island of Sumatra. It was painted in blues, greens and browns to represent the features of the terrain, and it seemed to be studded with many slim wooden rods.

"May I ask you first to look at these specimens," said Trelawney, indicating a display cabinet on one wall. We did so, and I gasped. Never have I seen such a collection of hypertropia. There were only four short shelves, but each contained a variety of broadly familiar, but outsized, biological specimens. There was, for example, a gigantic snail, fully nine inches long, embalmed in a jar of formaldehyde. There were several leaves framed and mounted; some were of tropical plants I did not recognise, but I recognised the sinusoidal outline of what would have been an oak leaf, had it not been almost a foot in length. There was the skull of a gigantic monkey; a pineapple that would have supplied a Lord Mayor's banquet; the desiccated corpse of a dung beetle as large as a cat, and other objects related only by their staggering size.

"All that you see here, gentlemen," Trelawney continued, after we had spent a little time considering these things, "was collected in a certain area of the island of Sumatra by my agent, Mr. Lee. He is a leading apothecary in Penang, and I entered correspondence with him many years ago when I sought his assistance in obtaining a certain rare plant that is effective in stimulating the appetite. One day, he sent me a specimen of that plant fully ten times the size of any other I had seen. He explained that in his travels into the interior of the island in search of additions to his stock, he had come across an area where, to his amazement, much of the flora and fauna had grown to gigantic size. I offered to pay him well for further examples, and although the spot is very difficult of access, has managed over the years to send me the examples you see here, as well as detailed reports on various matters.

"You will observe that the whole natural kingdom is represented: plants, insects, reptiles, mammals and man himself. From this I deduce that giantism is not an inherited trait; rather it must be stimulated by some feature of the environment."

"This skull, then," I interrupted, pointing to the object I had taken to be from an enormous ape, "is that of a man?"

"Yes, indeed. The structure of the cranium leaves no doubt: it is a previously unknown example of early man, grown to giant size and very possibly the origin of our present-day legends of similar beings.[1]

"To continue, then: having reached the conclusion that this area harboured conditions which encouraged increased growth, I spared no effort in finding what they might be. At last, after instructing the invaluable Mr. Lee to carry out investigations on many aspects of the site, I believe I have discovered the active substance." Trelawney paused in triumph.

"Can it be pitchblende?" asked Holmes.

Trelawney looked somewhat crestfallen. "I see your reputation is not exaggerated, Mr. Holmes. Yes, it is indeed a very rich lode of the substance pitchblende that I believe to be responsible. Small quantities of it will be leached into the surrounding soil by the rains, and so taken up by plants. These will be eaten by herbivorous animals, which will in turn be eaten by carnivores. I have at last obtained a good supply of pitchblende, which I have stored in my cellars. What remains is for me to conduct a series of experiments to establish at what age, under what conditions and in what quantities the pitchblende must be administered. I expect my live specimen, the rat, to provide vital data in this. Once I have completed this task, which surely cannot take longer than a year or two, we will be able to breed giants at will."

"This is of enormous scientific interest, of course," I ventured, "but surely it cannot cause the revolution you speak of?"

---

[1] In 1941 the anthropologist, Von Koenigswald, discovered the skull of a giant on the neighbouring island of Java. He named the specimen *Meganthropus javanicus*. It seems from this evidence that it originated in Sumatra - Editor.

Trelawney looked at me in astonishment. "Can you not see, Dr. Watson, what a difference this will make to the lives of the common man? When one giant pig or one giant lamb will feed dozens, or a few ears of giant wheat will suffice for an entire loaf, we will have banished hunger from the world forever. And when the great mass of people are freed from the need to spend their time earning enough to eat, will we not see a leap forward in artistic and scientific development? I tell you solemnly, gentlemen, we are on the verge of a golden age!"

All that we had seen and heard filled us with excitement. We spent the next hours with Dr. Trelawney in his drawing room discussing the implications of his discovery further and toasting him in several glasses of a fine old brandy. Finally, a little before dawn, we took our leave and walked the short distance to Baker Street. There we slept the deep sleep due to us at the end of a long and successful investigation.

We heard no more from Dr. Trelawney, although I watched the papers for signs that he was ready to give his findings to the world. It was a year later when we were sitting at the breakfast table, that Sherlock Holmes passed me a letter.

"You will find this of interest, Watson," he said. Then rising to his feet, he began pacing the room, as was his habit when in deep thought. The missive ran as follows:

'DEAR SHERLOCK HOLMES,

'As you and Dr. Watson are the only other people that are aware of the direction of my work, I felt I should write to you in order to warn you of the dreadful dangers that await anyone who tries to repeat my experiments.

'After many failed attempts, I realised that ingestion of pitchblende under any conditions made no difference to the development of an animal. Later, after much experimentation, I made the vital discovery that if a pregnant female is left in the presence of a large quantity of the substance, she will give birth to malformed young. On rare occasions indeed these were giants, but more often they were grotesque monsters of various kinds: some with two heads; some with no limbs; some of every horror that can be imagined.

'Most of these creatures did not live long, and I can only suppose that conditions in the dense growth of the Sumatran jungle favoured the large beasts, so that by natural selection they were the ones that predominated. Or it may well be that Mr. Lee, seeing the direction of my interest, did not choose to tell me of the monsters.

'At any event, I have made a further discovery regarding the nature of this variety of pitchblende: I have developed cancer, and my physician informs me that I have only weeks to live. It is my conclusion that the influence that emanates from the substance changes the natural course of development. In some cases this results in the anomalous growth of a foetus and in others precipitates the fate that has befallen me. The effects appear to be entirely random.

'I have destroyed my notes and specimens, including the giant rat, which I poisoned and disposed of in a hospital incinerator.

'As my last request, I ask you to continue to keep your counsel for as long as seems necessary to you, but if you should hear of any experimenter who chances to follow in my steps, I ask you to put before him what you know.

'Yours faithfully,

'ABRAHAM TRELAWNEY'

"This is most remarkable, Holmes!" I exclaimed.

"Indeed it is, Watson. The concept of an invisible and malignant emanation is a terrifying one. Let us hope that one day man will be able to tame and control it. That day will certainly be far distant, so let us follow the request of the unfortunate Dr. Trelawney, and keep our counsel."

THE ADVENTURE OF THE GYPSY GIRL

recall that one summer's day I was conversing with Sherlock Holmes in our lodgings in Baker Street. Glancing down from the window that overlooks that road, I observed a fashionable carriage draw up, pulled by a pair of handsome bays. The coachman leaped from his place and handed down a young lady dressed in the height of fashion.

Sherlock Holmes lifted his eyebrows. "It seems we are to be honoured with a visit from the quality, Watson. I trust it will not turn out to be some silly or trivial matter. She has certainly come from Hampstead at a good pace."

"Hampstead?" I queried.

"I believe so," returned my friend. "Notice the state of the horses – far from fresh, although not muddy, so from within London. But a young lady of that class does not rise early so they have been set a good pace for a few miles. The direction of arrival indicates the north, and her obvious prosperity indicates a fashionable area, therefore we have Hampstead."

A short while later the young lady was shown into our room. "Which of you is Mr. Sherlock Holmes?" she inquired in a voice that was serious in tone although not perceptibly distraught.

Holmes bowed. "Won't you take a seat, madam?" he asked, "and tell us in proper order what it is that concerns you."

"Thank you sir," she said seating herself. "I should first tell you that I am Lady Arabella Middlethorpe, daughter of Lady Headfort. My father, the Marquess of Headfort, as you may be aware, died some years ago and I live with mamma in Hampstead. At present, the marchioness is most unfortunately away in Buxton taking the waters and I did not know whom to turn to for advice, but then I recalled your fame and came here at once.

"The matter concerns a young friend of mine, a gypsy girl in fact, who has mysteriously disappeared. I greatly fear some harm has come to her and I would like to engage you to find her."

A look of polite weariness crossed my friend's face. "Surely, madam," he said, "you concern yourself without need. The gypsy folk are well able to take care of themselves, and often find themselves in need of leaving a locality at short notice."

"You do not take me seriously," she said with a hauteur I found charming, "but I tell you that to my certain knowledge and experience dark deeds are afoot! I first met Isobel Lee about three weeks ago. Her family were encamped in the Vale of Health not far from my home. She was telling fortunes in the street and as I know that gypsy women often have the second sight I asked for a reading." Her voice lowered in awe. "And I tell you sirs, it was nothing less than uncanny – she knew secrets of my past I had forgotten myself. She knew my entire situation. She described my friends and acquaintances to the life, although she could never have met them."

I said nothing, but I thought to myself it would not be difficult to deceive this credulous and rather foolish girl with a few generalities and dark hints.

She continued her story. "She said she would read my future, and as she looked at my palm I saw her eyes grow wide with shock. She told me earnestly that I would be in great danger on three separate occasions in the near future. The first occasion she said was very near. I should beware when travelling as she believed that was where the danger was at its height. Fortunately, she had on her person a charm against harm. She gave it to me and earnestly urged me to wear it constantly about my neck." The girl now put her hands to her dainty neck and withdrew a small silver charm on a thin chain.

I bent forward and examined it. "Ah, yes, Joan of Cornwall is it not?" I said this rather mischievously, as I

28

could see that Sherlock Holmes was aghast at this waste of his time.

"It is, sir. I tipped her well and was careful to wear it as she suggested. The next day I was riding on my nag Betsy across an unmade path on the Heath, when without warning the horse stumbled and reared. I feared it would roll on me, and perhaps cause serious hurt, because unluckily we were at the worst possible point, where the path skirted a deep dell. I would almost certainly have been injured, but I thought instantly of my charm and grabbed it in one of my hands and the horse recovered itself. The outcome was a happy one, but you can imagine how it affected me."

Holmes expression modified at this, "An interesting coincidence," he remarked. "Was this path a favourite ride of yours?"

"Oh yes, Mr. Holmes. It gives a wonderful view over the West End and the City and I ride there perhaps three times a week."

"I understand. Please go on."

"As you will appreciate, I sought out Isobel at once. Fortunately she was still to be found in the village, telling fortunes and selling clothes pegs and other small items to support her family. I told her of my escape, and she was most relieved and congratulated me on my good fortune. I asked her to take tea with me at my home, which she kindly did. Of course I thanked her again and again, and now that I had proof of her second sight, I besought her to tell me of the other occasions when I might be in danger. She decided to use the tea leaves on that occasion, and asked me to swirl the dregs of my cup about and empty them into a saucer. She then studied the marks and traces left by the tea leaves, which is a very powerful guide to those gifted enough to see it."

All this was said with complete assurance. I smiled and was amused to see my friend roll his eyes to the ceiling.

"The leaves, gentlemen, told her that my second occasion of danger was upon me." She paused dramatically. "I was in danger of a physical attack! Naturally, I vowed instantly not to set a foot out of doors, but Isobel advised against this course. What would happen, would happen she said, and there was no avoiding fate. However, she said that she would again give me protection against it. She took the charm from me and held it close in her hands, muttering some words in the Romany tongue, and then she returned it saying that she had imbued it with protection against the evil of mankind.

"A few days later I happened to be coming home alone from Hampstead High Street. It was only a short way from my home and I was on foot. There were few people about, perhaps because it was around dinner time, but I had no intimation of danger. But then, as I passed the corner of the Frognal where as you may know there is little view in any direction, a rough unshaven fellow lurched out at me. The vicious expression on his face almost froze my blood. I was convinced my last hour had come, but again I bethought me of my charm and snatched it out from my neck and held it out at him. I can see you are sceptical, gentlemen, but here was the proof. As soon as the ruffian saw the charm he let out a hoarse cry, stumbled back and ran off as fast as his legs would carry him. I could not longer have the smallest doubt of Isobel's accuracy and benevolence towards me."

As the recital continued, Holmes began to look more interested. I also was fascinated: how could the gypsy girl have predicted all this? The attack of course could well have been collusion, although it was difficult to see what could be gained by such a ruse, but how could she know a horse would stumble? I leant forward to listen attentively to her story.

"Again I sought out Isobel and invited her to visit me. There I gave her two gold sovereigns: a tidy sum, but surely no more than my life was worth. And of course I was desperate to know about the third danger and how I might avoid it.

"Isobel took out a set of Tarot cards that she said she had been given by her great-grandmother, a famous seer among the Romany people. She asked me to lay the pack to my forehead then took the cards and shuffled them well. Then she dealt out four cards in the pattern known as the Celtic Cross and asked me to pick one out. When I turned over the first one, I almost swooned – it was the skeleton, gentlemen: the symbol of death!"

Lady Arabella gracefully leaned her head back and breathed deeply with the recollection of it. "I was almost in despair and could hardly bear to go on, but Isobel insisted and I made another choice. The next card was almost as terrifying – it was the Tower: a tower riven by lightning in the darkness. Next I turned over the Empress of Cups and finally the Moon.

"Isobel explained their significance. Death indicated great danger; the tower was my own home; the Empress was myself and the moon sign gave the time. She said that the danger of death hung over all of us at Headfort Hall. The moon was waning at the time, and on Saturday when it was no longer to be seen, death would come to the house! She could not be completely certain who would be struck down she said; it was very likely to be myself, but it was possibly to be one of the servants. I implored her to take the charm again and imbue it with a counter-spell but she said it was not possible. Where the moon goddess herself was concerned, no charm could stand against her."

"I take the point," said Holmes dryly. "So naturally you moved the entire household out for the night?"

She looked startled, "Why however did you know that?" she asked, then recollected herself with a charming smile, "oh of course, I'm being foolish: to a great detective such as yourself this must have been obvious."

"Please do not describe yourself as foolish, madam," murmured Holmes. "Please go on – I take it that the house was mysteriously ransacked in your absence?"

'IT WAS THE SKELETON, GENTLEMEN: THE SYMBOL OF DEATH!'

The girl looked puzzled for an instant, then laughed, "Ah, Mr. Holmes, what a cynic you are! I see you think it was all a gypsy plot to get us out of the house for the night. No indeed, nothing was disturbed. I took rooms at the local inns for myself and such of the household that required them.

Fortunately not many were needed, for many of our staff live out and others are in Buxton with my mother. We all returned early the next morning and found everything exactly as we had left it.

"Naturally my first act was to seek out Isobel to thank her and talk to her, but to my surprise she was nowhere to be found. I went to the gypsy encampment personally and everyone denied knowledge of her and furthermore no-one seemed very concerned about her disappearance. They just shrugged and said they 'reckoned she had decided to flit.' I could get nothing out of them. It was very vexing. I always understood that gypsy folk stood by each other, but I saw nothing of that."

"And so madam, you would like us to find this girl?"

"If it is at all possible, Mr. Holmes. Expense is not an objection; I am not a poor woman and would spend anything to rescue a friend who has saved my life not once, but three times!"

"Your attitude does you credit, madam," said Holmes. "Well, I believe I will take your case. It does have some interesting features. I would like to see the scenes of the incidents for myself and draw what conclusions I may. May we call on you, Lady Arabella; at shall we say ten thirty tomorrow morning?"

The next day we presented ourselves at Headfort Hall. The young lady was waiting for us in her walking clothes and we set out across the Heath. After a stroll of perhaps three-quarters of a mile we came to the spot where she had almost been thrown on the first occasion. It was clear even to me from the churned ground that the horse had acted wildly.

"If you would both be so good as to stand back," said Holmes, "I would like to investigate in detail." He meticulously covered the ground, crouched down with his eyes scanning the grass. A few times he lifted small objects for consideration. Most he tossed back, but I saw him pocket a couple. At last he straightened and returned to where we were standing.

"If you will forgive us, Lady Arabella," he said, "I would like to consult with my colleague." He drew me a little aside, took out some small, mottled brown objects from his pocket and held them out for my inspection. "I believe I have made a certain amount of progress, Watson," he announced. "Take a look at these."

"Simply horse-chestnut fruit," I said. "Surely they are not unusual in this area?"

"Come, Watson," reproved my friend. "Do you see any chestnut trees close by? And if they should be brought here, say by a small boy playing conkers, would they not have rotted by this time of year? Also, close observation will show you these have been dried by a fire or on a stove to make them much harder than in nature."

"I see!" I exclaimed, "They were planted on the path to make the horse rear!"

"That is the obvious conclusion. Someone knew of Lady Arabella's habits and scattered the burrs a short while before she arrived and at a point where when the horse shied it would be likely to lose its footing."

"A gypsy trick, then?" I suggested. "They are traditionally skilful in their knowledge of horseflesh."

"Certainly," nodded Sherlock Holmes. "It is clear that Isobel Lee made sure that her predictions would come to pass. We know further that she had at least one accomplice because he took the part of Lady Arabella's attacker a few days later. Perhaps he was a brother or cousin; the matter would be simple to arrange. The deck of cards of course was stacked – long practice would have enabled her to deal what cards she chose."

We rejoined Lady Arabella, who led us back to the village and showed us the spot where she had been threatened. There was little to observe except that what she had said about it being a spot that could not easily be overlooked was true. Holmes asked then if he could make an investigation at Headfort Hall itself.

"I normally take coffee at this time," she announced on our arrival. "Will you gentlemen join me while we discuss the matter further?"

"With the greatest of pleasure," replied Holmes, bowing.

We seated ourselves in the morning room and talked of inconsequential matters. After a short wait the parlour-maid brought us a tray bearing a highly ornate silver coffee pot, as well as the fine china and other necessities. When Lady Arabella had poured coffee for us all, Holmes continued with his questions.

"Now, Lady Arabella," he began, "I understand from what you have told us that Isobel Lee only visited this house on a single occasion?"

"That is correct, Mr. Holmes," replied the young lady. "I received her in this very room."

"Did you spend the whole time here?"

"No, sir. After the reading, she most kindly offered to go around the house and bless all the rooms. She recited an incantation in the gypsy language that was sure to bring good luck."

"I see," mused my friend. "Perhaps you would be kind enough to take myself and Dr. Watson on the same tour of this building, in as exact manner as you can recall."

"If you wish, sir," said the girl, apparently puzzled, "but I cannot see how this will help your investigations."

"Nevertheless, madam, if you would oblige me I may be able to gain some information, and if you could recall any incident at any point please share it with us."

After finishing our coffee, the girl showed us the rooms of the house, all of which were well-furnished but largely in a rather old-fashioned manner, no doubt corresponding to the date of her parents' marriage. She gave us such details as she recalled, but apparently Isobel Lee had spoken little beyond the words of her blessing.

At one point we came to a relatively small room on the ground floor, partly furnished for comfort but also showing unmistakable signs of business activities.

"What is this room used for?" asked Sherlock Holmes.

"This is mamma's private room," replied Lady Arabella. "She relaxes here with an improving volume in the evenings, and transacts such household business as is necessary."

"That is a handsome piece of furniture," said Holmes, indicating a mahogany item against one wall. It was in the Regency style, and seemed to me to be a desk topped by a breakfront bookcase.

"That is mamma's desk; she writes all her letters from there."

Holmes peered at it more closely. "Yes, I believe it to be the work of George Smith. Made perhaps about seventy years ago."

"That may well be, sir," said the girl. "I know little of these matters."

"One characteristic of Smith's work," persisted my friend, "is his fondness for secret compartments. Does this example have one?"

"Not to my knowledge," said the girl.

"Well, let us see," said Holmes, pulling a measuring tape from his pocket.

For some minutes he darted about the piece of furniture in the manner characteristic of him: now crouching down; now stretching up; measuring sides; pulling out drawers and measuring them in all three dimensions, muttering figures to himself as he did so. Finally, he gave a muted exclamation of triumph and completely pulled out one drawer of a row of four. He reached into the back of the recess thus formed. He appeared to tug at something which did not give. He paused for a moment; thought, then pulled out the drawer to the left a little way. He reached in again and tugged gently, apparently feeling the nature of the resistance. Then he pulled out the drawer on the other side and this time was able to extract and display for us a small box.

"Here we are," said Holmes with satisfaction. "A clever scheme, worthy of Smith at his best. The compartment is behind one drawer, but it can only be removed if both adjoining drawers are at least partly opened. Now let us see what we have here."

We all clustered round the box, which I noted was not dusty – Lady Headfort must have been in the habit of using the hidden compartment, but knowing her daughter's careless and talkative ways had decided not to take her into the secret.

From the box he lifted a long, narrow jewel case.

"The emeralds!" cried Lady Arabella at once, lifting her hands to her mouth.

Holmes opened the case and showed us that it was empty. "Can you cast any light on this, madam?" he asked.

"The case," stammered the girl, "it is the one in which mamma keeps the family emerald necklace – a most valuable piece. My grandfather obtained it many years ago when he was commanding his regiment in Egypt, but she would not take her best jewels to Buxton: there are no social occasions there worthy of them."

"Where, then, are they usually kept?"

"I don't know," fluttered the girl. "Perhaps there; where you have found them."

"It seems, then, that the emeralds have been stolen," said my friend.

"Oh no, this is dreadful!" exclaimed the girl. "My mother will be prostrate, and she will blame me! Oh, that vile, treacherous girl! How could I have trusted her?"

"I greatly fear your conclusion is correct, madam," said Holmes, "There can be little doubt that Isobel Lee also knows something about secret compartments and arranged for the house to be empty in order that she could investigate the matter."

"Oh, Mr. Holmes," cried the girl, "you must help me! The emeralds are part of my inheritance and mamma would never allow me to forget the matter as long as she lives! Is there anything to be done?"

Holmes made a *moué*. "I cannot conceal from you, madam, that that will be no easy task. A single gypsy girl will have no difficulty in losing herself in the teeming millions of London, and there are many ready markets for fine jewels."

To my distress Lady Arabella began to cry. I hurried to her side in an effort to comfort her.

Holmes insisted on completing the tour, despite Lady Arabella's unhappiness. In one room at the rear of the house, Holmes pointed out the loose catch on one of the window sashes and the marks where it had been forced. The gypsy would have course have had unlimited time to search the premises.

"But why did she not simply strip the house?" I asked.

"Come, Watson, surely you would not expect a gypsy to carry a Sheraton sideboard in a caravan? Your gypsy is a traditionalist: he favours small valuable items that are easily secreted and easily sold, snuffboxes and the like. Jewels are most desirable, although naturally hard to come by."

When we had completed our tour, Holmes asked if he might interview the housekeeper. We were led to the housekeeper's room and introduced to Mrs. Simpson, an elderly but obviously competent and experienced woman.

"May I ask," said my friend after some preliminary remarks, "if you were aware of the visit of the gypsy girl on the occasion when she took tea with Lady Arabella?"

"I was, sir," returned the housekeeper, "and I cannot say that I was very pleased with the matter – nasty, thieving lot that they are – but it is not my place to dictate who the family will receive at Headfort Hall."

Holmes made a gesture of understanding. "The gypsy folk are notorious for petty theft, Mrs. Simpson. In this particular case, did you notice any pilfering?"

Mrs. Simpson drew herself up. "I did, sir. Two of the teaspoons were missing after her visit. I told Lady Arabella of course, but she dismissed the idea and said that I must have miscounted."

"A few days later, I believe you were asked to move out for the night?"

Mrs. Simpson's grim expression did not soften in the slightest. "I was, sir. A room was reserved for me at the Bull and Bush a short way from here. It was comfortable enough, I suppose, but not what I am used to. I had to share the room with Ellie; one of the maids."

"Quite so, and on your return, did you notice anything amiss?"

"No, I did not," replied the housekeeper, somewhat reluctantly. "I did inspect the premises of course, as is my duty, but I could see nothing wrong or out of place. No harm was done, even if the scheme was –" she hesitated, "– somewhat eccentric."

Holmes had no further questions, and after some words of thanks we withdrew for a discussion. Holmes seemed cautiously pleased. "The girl could not resist stealing the teaspoons, Watson! This could be our first line of enquiry. Do you recall the silverware when we took coffee? No? It was of the King's Pattern, a highly ornate and distinctive design, and furthermore as it was introduced only this century it is not as widespread as more traditional patterns. I also glanced at the hallmark – a crown and a lion, the marks of the Sheffield silversmiths – not so often found in London: again a stroke of luck. I believe Watson, that those teaspoons may be Isobel Lee's downfall!"

We took our leave of the distraught Lady Arabella, and as we travelled back to Baker Street my friend gave me some of his thoughts.

"The case is not quite hopeless, Watson. Emeralds in themselves are of no use to a gypsy: they must be turned into hard cash. Normally the Romany folk are most reluctant to mix with the *gajo*, as they call us: you will never see a gypsy in a padding-ken. But in cases such as this they are compelled to go outside their tribe to find a dealer who is able to dispose of their plunder.

"Now, the number of fences who could handle such valuable items is severely limited. It is a mistake to believe that all receivers of stolen goods are like Mr. Dickens' Fagin – low fellows in sordid surroundings dealing in handkerchiefs and coal scuttles stolen from areas and suchlike. The true aristocracy of crime will have no dealing with such trash. They will go to ostensibly respectable dealers in valuable articles – and indeed most of their trade is respectable – who are not averse to earning important sums from buying stolen items at a fraction of their true value.

"Silver and gold can be melted in the dealer's crucibles. Gems can be re-cut and re-set so that their owner will never know them. Then they can be sold in perfect safety at an enormous profit.

"The situation is more complex with ornate items, where the true value is in the craftsmanship. The dealer will attempt to sell discreetly where he can. Even here, he runs little risk. If anything should be discovered, why he has the name and address of the seller, which to his shock and dismay are false. He makes no trouble in returning goods proven to be stolen, protesting that his good name is of the first essence."

"What of the emeralds?" I asked. "Will they be re-cut?"

"I believe re-cutting is unlikely and unnecessary," replied my friend, "because such stones are almost always shaped into the traditional square cut. It is however very likely that the necklace will be broken up into individual items such as rings or brooches, and in such a case proving the original ownership would be impossible.

"We must seek first at Hatton Garden, the traditional centre of the jewellery trade. I believe Isobel Lee will have gone there with her tale of emeralds. Our task is to read her mind as she reads others, and find the shop she chose."

"But will she run this errand herself, Holmes?" I asked. "Perhaps she asked a brother or cousin to take the risk."

"Perhaps," replied Sherlock Holmes, "but I think not. Certainly gypsies trust their family first, and we know she had at least one accomplice. But in this case, where the haul is so valuable I believe she would not even tell her family; not because she cannot trust them not to cheat her, but because she would be pestered for a share of the profits.

"Further, the girl believes herself safe from pursuit; she will not be in a hurry to strike a deal. The negotiations for such a sum will take time. I believe we have a little time before they are concluded. If we work quickly and have luck we may be successful.

We lunched in Soho and afterwards walked back to our lodgings. There we relaxed in armchairs, Holmes languidly puffing on a cigarette as he pondered. Finally, he spoke: "I fear Watson that we are in for a spell of drudgery – the sort of task that I would normally leave to the regular police force. However, our client does not wish the matter to be public knowledge, so we must do it ourselves. To Hatton Gardens, Watson! There we will visit the most likely jewellers and see what we can find."

We took a cab to Hatton Garden and as we strolled along that thoroughfare I found the scale of the undertaking daunting. "But Holmes," I protested, "there must be well over a hundred shops here, and no doubt more in the surrounding streets. We cannot possibly check them all in the time we have!"

"Quite right," said my friend, "but I think we can eliminate many if not most from our enquiries. The larger shops all have numerous employees and there they would not dare to deal in doubtful items as the honest members of staff would be sure to find out in time what they are up to. We will visit only those with a single shopkeeper on duty."

This scheme bought the matter to manageable proportions, leaving us with about twenty shops each to visit. While I took the east side of the street, Holmes took the west.

I walked along the thoroughfare visiting each of the smaller shops in turn, and eventually came to a small establishment near Greville Street. I entered the rather dingy interior and delivered what was by now a well-practised speech.

"I am trying to replace a teaspoon of this pattern," I said to the shopkeeper, producing one we had borrowed from Headfort Hall. "Our maid has carelessly lost one of a set. I would like to match it as closely as can be done, and I would also like to match the hallmark if at all possible."

The proprietor bowed. "You show the meticulousness of a true connoisseur, sir," he remarked fawningly. "If one might see the item?"

I handed it over for his inspection. "I have a few King's Pattern items in stock, sir," he said after a glance at the hallmark, "and if you would kindly wait a few moments I will see what I can do."

He left me and went into the back of the shop, returning in a short while with a box of cutlery. He sorted out the teaspoons and laid them on the counter. "This is what we have, sir. Now, let us look at the hallmarks. Screwing a glass into his eye he held each spoon up to the light in turn.

"Ah!" he said after quizzing a few. "I am fortunately able to oblige you, sir. The Crown mark of Sheffield as you require. Let me show you them both together: as like as two peas wouldn't you say?"

"Certainly," I agreed. "I will purchase it at once."

"There is a second one here, sir, with the same hallmark. Perhaps you would like a spare in case of future accidents?"

I considered for a moment, then agreed – it would be pleasant to restore as much of Lady Arabella's property as possible.

He wrapped the spoons, which I carried in triumph back to Holmes.

"Excellent work, Watson!" exclaimed Sherlock Holmes, examining the spoons discreetly. "I see the jeweller has cleaned them, so removing the patina and robbing me of most of my data, but the amounts of wear correspond closely, and taken with a hallmark which is not often found in London, and the fact that he had exactly two spoons of this type I believe that it is almost certain that this is the shop that Isobel Lee chose. We have taken an immense step forward: where she sold the spoons will be where she fences the jewels."

"Might she not already have done so?"

"If so, the matter becomes simple: we will pass our information on to the regular police who will have enough evidence to raid the premises. However, I think such valuable goods will require more time to strike a deal than has elapsed. We will therefore now attempt to work from the other end: by tracing the girl herself!"

"A difficult matter surely?" I said doubtfully.

"Well, we will do what we can. Would you do me the kindness to return to Baker Street tomorrow morning? And as we will not be moving in the best circles, would you dress in working-men's clothes?"

After breakfast the next day, I returned to Holmes' lodgings to find him disguised as a gypsy. He had dyed his hair black and tinted his skin with walnut juice to give a swarthy look. In addition, he had omitted to shave that morning so there was visible stubble on his chin. He had donned the everyday clothes of that class and wore a red neckerchief at the throat. I myself wore a serviceable old suit and cloth cap that I had used before when accompanying Holmes in the less salubrious parts of town.

"I hope you find this convincing, Watson?" he asked cheerfully. "It is not after all such a difficult disguise. If you are ready, we will find a cab and see if I can also convince others of the gypsy tribe."

We took a cab to Fleet Street, then dismounted and walked southwards towards the river. As we walked,

Holmes explained his reasoning: "Isobel Lee will wish to remain out of sight but at the same time not too far from her receiver. I am guessing that this means she will stay for a time in Southwark, where questions are not asked of a stranger and where lodgings are cheap. With a little trouble I think we may find someone that knows her."

I looked dubious. "But Holmes, if we make any sort of enquiry ourselves, will not word of it get back to the girl very quickly?"

"Quite right Watson, which is why we will not ask questions, but rather send her a message. I am fortunate in that I speak a smattering of the Romany tongue, following a period in my early career when I lived for a time with a travelling circus. Luckily for us the language is very degenerate in England – only about three thousand words are in use – compared to the purer gypsy tongues of central Europe."

We crossed Blackfriars Bridge and found ourselves immediately in a slum district. The buildings were grimy and in ill repair. Many windows were smashed and crudely covered with wood or sheet metal. From somewhere nearby came the noisome smell of a tannery.

We idled along, as if we were working men who had no employment. On several occasions we espied men with the look of a gypsy, whereupon Holmes would go up to them and say: "*Sarshin, prala. Jinnes tu the chavali Isobel Purrum, ava acoi collico?*" – Greetings, brother, do you know the girl Isobel Lee, who has come here recently?

One man shook his head in bafflement; two said: "*Ne, prala.*" – No, brother. But the fourth person we approached, a young handsome fellow with a gold ring in his ear, made the reply: "*Ava, prala.*" – I do, brother.

"*Boro pukker-engri se mande.*" – I have an important message for her – said my friend.

"*So se lis?*" – What is it?

44

"*Kinnipen koshto. She jal av rashengro-stadj kitchema tarsarla a desch ora.*" – The price is agreed. She is to go to the Mitre[1] this evening at ten o'clock.

"*Deavlis lesti.*" – I will tell her.

Holmes gave the gypsy a small coin, which was accepted with a nod of thanks.

"One last step Watson, and our trap is set. Let us return to Hatton Garden."

We walked back over the river to Hatton Garden, a stroll of no more than twenty minutes. I indicated to Holmes the shop where I had purchased the teaspoons, keeping well clear of the window as I did so. My friend entered the shop but rejoined me a few moments later.

"Back to Baker Street, Watson," he said on his return. "I simply told the fellow that the 'lady with the emeralds' would like to talk to him at the Mitre – a nearby public house convenient for our purposes – tonight at ten. He showed no surprise. I believe he will be there: such jewels as those would entice him to take a little trouble. Further, as our message to Isobel Lee was that the price is agreed we can be confident she will bring the jewels with her. Now we need only make arrangements for her reception. I must send a telegram."

At Baker Street, a surprise awaited us. Lady Arabella had paid us a visit. Mrs. Hudson, delighted to be able to socialise with the aristocracy, was entertaining her in her own drawing room with tea and conversation. Lady Arabella was initially taken aback at our entrance, as we still wore our disguises, but recovered herself when Holmes bowed and addressed her.

"We have been busy upon your affairs, madam, and we believe we have made significant progress," he said.

"Oh, Mr. Holmes, I pray you are successful! Please forgive this intrusion, which I know can be of no help, but I have been unable to rest or relax from worry!"

---

[1] Lit. Priest's-hat alehouse – Editor.

"I quite understand, madam," said Holmes. "It so happens that we may be able to recover the gems this very night. We have made certain arrangements, which we believe will bring Isobel Lee to a certain spot."

"Oh, Mr. Holmes!" exclaimed Lady Arabella. "If you manage to restore the jewels I will be forever in your debt!"

Sherlock Holmes bowed his acknowledgement. "Perhaps, Lady Arabella," he said, "you would be interested in coming with us tonight? It is not essential, but your identification of the girl will save us time at a moment when speed is vital."

"I would be very happy to accompany you!"

"Then may I ask you to join us here at nine o'clock this evening, dressed in the clothes of one of your maids?"

"Certainly. I will not disturb your work any longer, and will return tonight." With that, and with gracious thanks to Mrs. Hudson for the refreshments, she left us.

"Now, Watson," said Holmes, "I will shave and change then I must send a telegram to a friend of mine in the Cambridgeshire constabulary."

"Cambridgeshire?" I replied, puzzled.

"Yes," said Holmes, "by one of those delightful freaks of English law, the Mitre comes under the jurisdiction of that county, as the premises were once the property of the Bishops of Ely. We must of course have the police present to carry out the arrest and charging, but the Metropolitan police have a tendency as a class to be impulsive and self-opinionated. I find it easier to work with officers of the rural forces."

By nine o'clock we were all assembled. A Sergeant Cole had arrived by train from Cambridge. At Holmes' request he had come wearing civilian clothes: a set of smart tweeds, which to my eye were a little countrified, but would no doubt pass unremarked in a crowd. He was a careful and stolid man with an air of authority. Lady Arabella was present in a blue dress and large shawl which she wore over her head. I had decided to retain the old suit and cap I had worn that morning in Southwark as the jeweller knew me as a gentleman.

We took a four-wheeler to Holborn, then walked the short distance to Ely Court in order to make an unostentatious arrival. We took our places in the Public Bar well before ten o'clock, at a table close to the door so as to be able to block the exit if necessary. We arranged matters so that Holmes and Lady Arabella sat facing the door and would give warning as the jeweller or the gypsy girl entered. Sergeant Cole and myself sat on the opposite side of the table.

We waited perhaps twenty minutes making quiet conversation, when Holmes gave us a small nod to indicate that the jeweller had arrived – about ten minutes before the hour. I risked a casual look round and saw him standing at the bar sipping uneasily at a pale ale. Some time passed. Ten o'clock came and went. I feared that the girl might not arrive – perhaps she had not got the message or perhaps she suspected a trap?

I need not have worried. A short time later I saw Lady Arabella duck further under her shawl and touch Holmes' arm. I saw a number of other men in the bar turn their heads to stare at the newcomer, and under cover of this I looked up to see a gypsy girl of striking appearance walk past. She was tall for a woman and handsome with a fierce beauty. She carried nothing in her hands and I could see no pouch at her belt. Perhaps, I surmised, she wore a bag on a cord around her neck. The girl glanced along the line of drinkers at the bar and spying the jeweller strode up to meet him.

Holmes rose, as did the rest of us. "Please stay back, Lady Arabella," he asked, "we three will confront the pair."

At the bar, events were moving rapidly. The couple had exchanged a few words and looked at each other in suspicion when they found their stories did not tally. Instinctively, both looked around: the man fearfully and the gypsy in anger. I fear they noticed my fixed gaze. The girl reacted with the swiftness of her tribe and darted towards the door. As she passed Holmes, he suddenly grabbed her by her right arm; thrust his hand into a placket in her skirt and ripped out a leathern bag from the large concealed pocket that female pickpockets commonly wear. The girl gave a scream of fury and tried to snatch at the bag, but Holmes held it well above her head.

Sergeant Cole came forward more deliberately and began to say; "I am a police officer, madam, and I must ask you to …" he got no further. With her free hand the girl snatched a long hatpin from her garments, probably kept for just such occasions as this, and stabbed him in the upper arm. He yelled and fell back. The gypsy twisted herself out of Holmes' grasp and made a dart for the opposite door that led to the Saloon Bar. I ran after her, but she eeled through the crowds too swiftly for me, although I could follow her progress from the shouts of anger as she caused men to spill their drinks. By the time we too had gained the street she was well down the narrow alleyway that leads to Ely Place, and when we reached that badly-lit thoroughfare she had disappeared.

I returned to the public bar where the sergeant was questioning the jeweller harshly. As I arrived the latter gave me a lambent look of fury, obviously recognising me from the previous day and deducing that I had a hand in the affair.

"How was I to know she was a thief?" he snarled to the policeman. "She told me they were handed down from her great-grandmother. How was I to know they were stolen?"

"Don't give me that, my lad," said the sergeant. "Her great-grandmother my hat! Of course you must of known they were stole!"

"I didn't, I tell you!"

After some minutes of this, the policeman gave up. He took Holmes and myself aside. "There's not much I can do sirs, if he sticks to his story," he said. "We've got no proof and precious little evidence. I'll take him down to Holborn station, where they've kindly given me permission to work, and we'll put him through it a bit, but unless he breaks – and I don't think he will – we can't hold him."

"No matter, sergeant," said Sherlock Holmes equably. "We can congratulate ourselves on at least some success. The force now knows of another receiver and can keep an eye on him and his visitors for the future and my client has her jewels back and moreover has learned some valuable lessons which will benefit her in later life. As for you Watson, I must ask you to be discreet on this occasion; it would not do for the marchioness to discover how close she came to losing her most treasured gems!"

THE ADVENTURE OF THE AMAZONIAN EXPLORER

 arrived at Baker Street one day, to find Sherlock Holmes deep in conversation with an elderly and distinguished-looking gentleman.

"Good morning, Watson!" cried my friend. "May I introduce Sir Joseph Dalton Hooker, the Director of the Royal Botanic Gardens at Kew."

I bowed respectfully. I recognised the name at once as being that of one of the most eminent men of science in the land. Sir Joseph gave me a short and rather suspicious nod in reply.

"I hope that we will not have too many people knowing the facts of this matter, Mr. Holmes," he growled. "My whole reason in coming to you is that I cannot risk putting all the facts before the police force."

"You need have no fear, Sir Joseph," said my friend in his most soothing manner. "Watson is my constant companion. He does admittedly often write sensationalised versions of my exploits, but at my request he will desist on this occasion."

"Certainly," I said at once. "Many of Sherlock Holmes' cases involve confidences, and I write nothing for publication in such circumstances."

Sir Joseph appeared somewhat mollified and said to me, "As I have just remarked to Mr. Holmes, I am here in connection with the recent death of John Anderson, the noted South American naturalist and explorer. He did a good deal of work for Kew Gardens both in the field and in this country and there are certain matters relating to his decease that I would like investigated with the utmost discretion."

Holmes put in a remark: "I saw the notice of his death in the papers two days ago. They spoke merely of an unspecified accident at his home."

"It was a most bizarre accident, Mr. Holmes: he was found dead in his conservatory. The immediate cause of death was loss of blood."

"He had cut himself severely?"

"No: I said it was bizarre. A number of the giant Amazonian leeches which he bred in the conservatory for scientific purposes had attached themselves to him and sucked enough of his blood to kill him."

"Good heavens!" I exclaimed. "What possible purpose could be served by breeding leeches of such a size and in such numbers?"

"Anderson was a man of science," said Sir Joseph reprovingly. "For the purposes of his studies he wished to recreate the conditions of the Amazon forest floor as closely as possible. To do this, he felt he had to have as much of the chain of life as was possible. He has imported the most common Amazonian insects, both flying and burrowing; the small creatures, lizards and so on, that feed off the insects, and on their death are eaten by them; the plants and fungi of the region which eventually provide rotting material and so on. Over the years he has introduced into his conservatory over three hundred separate species of plant and animal life. It is in a sense a living laboratory."

"I begin to understand," I said, "and it is a remarkable and ambitious experiment. But surely death from the cause you describe is most unusual? When I was at Netley, taking the course prescribed for army surgeons, there was instruction in tropical diseases and I was told that leeches did not pose a threat to the actual life of a grown man."

"That is generally true," nodded Sir Joseph. "There are documented cases of men getting drunk in leech habitats and being found dead the next morning, but in general the leeches will be noticed and can easily be removed with salt or a hot coal."

"And is there any evidence he was drunk or drugged?" asked Holmes.

"I cannot be completely certain, as I know only what I have been told by his wife and servants. I can however state that it would be completely out of character. I have known him for many years and know that he drank only a little wine and took no drugs."

"It is quite certain that he was alone in the conservatory?"

"Absolutely. The door was locked on the inside, and his assistant had to smash a pane of glass to gain entry."

Holmes steepled his fingers. "It is certainly a bizarre occurrence as you say, Sir Joseph, but one might postulate an attack of dizziness or something similar that would leave a man vulnerable to such an attack. What leads you to consult myself, rather than a physician?"

Sir Joseph looked uneasy. "The police have already reached the conclusion you outline, Mr. Holmes. They have found that he suffered from malaria as a consequence of his travels, and believe that he fainted from this cause and died when the leeches drained his blood. There will of course be an inquest, but as there are no signs of any attack and the door was locked they expect a formal verdict of accidental death and are not looking for any third party. I must admit the evidence is compelling, but there are certain circumstances that make me wish to have the death investigated more thoroughly."

"And these are?" murmured Holmes, as Sir Joseph paused.

Sir Joseph's look of unease deepened, then he continued: "You will be aware, gentlemen, that up to about twenty years ago, the country of Brazil had a monopoly on rubber production. This was a major part of their economy and they were determined to keep it to themselves. The most severe penalties were introduced for anyone trying to export the seeds or young plants. Then in 1876 it was announced that a young adventurer, Henry Wickham, had brought some thousands of seeds of the species *Hevea* to us at Kew. We succeeded in germinating many of them and now of course Britain has extensive rubber plantations in her tropical colonies, to the great advantage of the Empire."

"I recall reading of Wickham's exploits as a young lad," I interjected heartily. "A splendid tale of British pluck and resource!"

Sir Joseph looked stony. "Indeed; that is the general opinion. The facts however are that the seeds were obtained by John Anderson and smuggled home by him in a mass of other specimens. By this means he was able to confound the Brazilian customs officials. He could not however have his own role in the matter made public as he would never again be able to return to the Amazon and his life's work would be at an end. Our consul found young Wickham who had been sent to Santerem in the upper Amazon by his family. In return for a sum of money, he agreed to take the credit for obtaining the seeds. A boastful person, he had a talent for self-publicity, and finally I do believe convinced himself that he was genuinely the man responsible. The joke was perhaps carried too far when he was later knighted for the exploit."

"I see," mused Holmes. "You think there may then be a possibility that the truth became known and a Brazilian patriot, or perhaps a ruined planter decided to assassinate Mr. Anderson?"

"I think it a distinct possibility."

"And yet, what advantage would accrue to them? And after so long a time the wounds would be less deep."

"Those of Iberian blood think little of advantage or of the lapse of years when honour is at stake. It is not uncommon for a man to spend his whole life to even a score."

"But you have not given this story to the police?"

"I cannot, Mr. Holmes. I simply cannot. The story of Wickham's exploits is so widespread. We would be scorned as liars. The Queen would be seen to have knighted someone wholly unworthy of the honour. So it is that I have come here in secret. I have told my staff that I have come to town to visit the Royal Society in connection with my duties there as its president."

Holmes leaned back in his chair. "As fascinating a problem as has come my way in many months, Sir Joseph. I thank you for bringing it to my attention. I will certainly take the case, and Watson and I will visit the scene of the incident tomorrow. I would be obliged if you could supply me with a letter of introduction to Mrs. Anderson, naming me perhaps as an expert in tropical diseases."

Sir Joseph wrote the letter at once at Holmes's writing desk. He then rose and bowed to us both. "I look forward to having your report as soon as possible Mr. Holmes," he said as he took his leave.

I arrived at Baker Street early the next morning at Holmes' request. As it was a fine day, we decided to eschew a cab and walked the mile to Paddington station. There we took the train for Kew Gardens station, near to which Anderson's house was situated.

We found the house without trouble. It was not in itself large, although no doubt more than adequate for a childless couple, but had extensive grounds going down to the river. We gave our names and the letter of introduction at the door, and a short while later a maid took us into her mistress's presence. Mrs. Anderson rose as we entered. She was a woman of striking appearance. Tall, dignified and with typical Iberian features, it was clear she had been the epitome of continental beauty in her youth. Indeed, that youth was not so far past: it was obvious that she was much younger than Anderson, who had been in his late fifties at the time of his death. She wore black, of course: her dress having many tucks and flounces and so on, rather than being in the plainer English style. We bowed in turn over her hand as she greeted us.

"Good morning gentlemen," she said. "Please be seated. I understand you are here to investigate the death of my poor husband." Her voice held a slight accent.

"We are indeed Madam," said Holmes, "and it is with profound sorrow that we trouble you at such a time, but you must understand that our investigations lose their force with time."

Mrs. Anderson shrugged. "I do not understand what the problem can be. My dear husband had been suffering from some dizzy spells lately, although he refused to go to the doctor. He said it was merely his old malarial trouble and he would dose himself with quinine. It is clear to me that he fainted while he was alone and so was killed by those repulsive creatures of his."

Holmes made a gesture of acquiescence. "That is almost certainly the case Madam, but of course we must follow the regulations in these matters."

"Of course. What can I help you with?"

"You spoke of malaria: was his health bad?"

She shrugged again. "The European is at a disadvantage in my country, Mr. Holmes. Disease is everywhere. Malaria; the yellow fever; dysentery; cholera: they all flourish in the hot climate. My Anderson spent much time in the Amazon. I first met him in Manaos, where my father was a government official. John came to him to get some papers. While in the town he fell ill of the fever. I acted as his nurse with the help of one of my servants, and through that we fell in love, although he was much older than I. In time we married and he brought me to London. Since then there have been other visits to Brazil and other illnesses. No, his health was never good."

I could not help breaking in at this point. "I trust you have friends and relatives to turn to, Mrs. Anderson? It would be intolerable for a widow to be alone in such circumstances."

Mrs. Anderson made an almost curt gesture of negation. "I have very few friends and no relations in this country. When the arrangements are made, I will return to my own people. I am tired of this cold wet city and the people who do not feel as we do. I long for the festivals; the dancing; the generous friendship that you will find in my own land." She indicated a large tapestry that hung in a prominent position. It was finely worked with a tropical scene: a tangle of jungle foliage profuse with large and brilliant flowers. A parrot perched on a branch, and a jaguar peered through the leaves. It had a savage beauty that I personally found a trifle unsettling. Mrs. Anderson stared at it for a while in silence. "I worked that tapestry myself gentlemen, and I love to look at it. It reminds me of my home, but at the same time it saddens me because I am so far from there."

"You have never returned to Brazil on one of your husband's expeditions?" asked Holmes.

"No: it is a very long way. I do not like the sea crossing and I cannot share my husband's interest in even the worms that writhe in the mud. Finally, they have killed him; he who kept them as if they were his pets."

"May we see his study?"

"Certainly." She rose and led us into an adjoining room fitted out as a study and library. Books on all aspects of natural history ranged the shelves. On the walls were mementoes, mainly of indian artefacts. A few examples of the taxidermist's art were also displayed: I recognised a tapir and an anteater with its distinctive long proboscis. It was generally tidy; Anderson obviously preferred to work neatly rather that scatter his paperwork about as is the custom with many men of science. On one corner of his desk was a large cabinet photograph of his wife as a young woman and on the other a matching photograph of an upright man in naval uniform.

"Who is that?" asked Holmes, indicating the latter.

Mrs. Anderson lifted an eyebrow. "That is the former King of Brazil; Dom Pedro. He befriended my husband in his younger days. The King was always most anxious to see the Amazon opened up to trade."

"He is no longer king?"

"No, he was deposed by the army. I believe he lives in France at present."

"Do you have Royalist sympathies, may I ask?"

She shrugged once more, "I am a woman: I take no interest in politics, and would not vote even if it were permitted. My husband had political views, although not strong ones."

"I see," murmured Holmes, "Perhaps we should now look at the scene of the tragedy."

"As you wish. I will not come with you. I cannot bear to think of that place. I will have it torn down as soon as this matter is over."

She rang a bell for the maid, who entered and dropped a curtsey. "Marie – take these gentlemen to Mr. Doggett and tell him to give them every assistance they require," she ordered.

We were taken to a small and crowded workroom at the rear of the house and introduced to Doggett, who described himself as Anderson's assistant and told us that he was the person who had originally raised the alarm. He was an alert young man, with obvious energy. After some preliminary questions, we asked him to take us to where he found the body. He led us to the foot of the gardens, close to the river, where there stood a very large conservatory, not ornate but stoutly built of white-painted wood. I noted that a small tributary channel lined with stone had been dug from the river upstream of the building; it passed under one wall and debouched at the other side. Across the Thames we could see the small and uninhabited Oliver's Island. It was a pleasant spot.

"This is our terrarium, as we call it, gentlemen," said Doggett. "It was designed by Mr. Anderson to mimic the conditions of the Amazon basin as closely as possible. As you may know, he had close connections with Kew Gardens and spent a good deal of time in the Palm House there studying its construction and heating methods. This door is the only entrance."

Mr. Doggett opened the door with his key. As we entered Holmes inspected the lock, which was of a simple rim design. Just inside the door were a wooden bench and some shelves holding various items of equipment and bottles of chemicals. A set of hooks and a pair of boots standing by the bench showed the area was used for changing. Beyond this, there was an apparently impenetrable tangle of plant growth. Nearby also there stood an enormous black cast-iron stove. The heat from this and the humidity of the place struck us at once.

"This stove is always kept burning, gentlemen," explained Doggett. "Although as it is so large, I only have to fill it twice a day. Once early in the morning and once in the late afternoon – we damp it down overnight. It serves to heat both the air and to take the chill off the water through some coils at the rear."

He led us along a narrow path in the undergrowth and after a few yards we arrived at the side of a sizeable pool. It was surrounded by jungle foliage of types unrecognisable to me. I could hear, but not see, small animals scuttling in the undergrowth. Many insects droned and buzzed about, some of them fully two inches long. One creature settled on me to drink my perspiration. I brushed it aside in instinctive revulsion. A small frog, vividly striped in yellow and black jumped abruptly off a rotted log as we approached the water's edge.

"This is where I found Mr. Anderson," said Doggett. "He was lying mainly under that bush, and with his feet in the pool. He was a terrible sight with the leeches stuck to him, all purple and swollen with his blood. A number of them had fastened on to the bare skin around his neck. It looked as if he were wearing some sort of heathen necklace. I dragged him at once to the entrance and ran for help. I brought salt back with me from the kitchen and got rid of the leeches, but it was all too late."

"HE WAS A TERRIBLE SIGHT WITH THE LEECHES STUCK TO HIM"

"And what time was this?" Holmes enquired.

"About seven o'clock in the evening, when I came to attend to the stove. His usual routine when in England was to visit the terrarium after lunch and spend the afternoon there. So I suppose he could have been lying there for up to five hours. When I arrived the door was fastened but I saw through the panes that the key was in the lock, so I knew he must be inside. I shouted and knocked on the glass but there was no reply. I feared some accident might have happened so I broke one of the panes in the door and reached through for the key."

Holmes nodded, and put another question: "Did he always work alone?"

"He preferred to work alone most of the time, sir. He said it was a habit he had got into during his time in the Amazon. He locked the door as well, partly to make sure he was undisturbed and partly to make sure members of the household didn't come in unescorted."

"Do you happen to know," asked Sherlock Holmes, "to what extent the Royal Botanic Gardens are involved in these experiments?"

"Mr. Anderson worked closely with Kew," replied Doggett, "but was entirely independent of them. He financed all his expeditions himself, and decided what areas to investigate. These researches were you might say his hobby, or perhaps better, his life's work. He told me often he considered himself a lucky man to have an absorbing interest and the means to indulge himself."

"He was a wealthy man then?"

"I couldn't exactly say, sir. There is no extravagance in the house, and very little entertaining, but on the other hand there is a sizeable household, and the expense of a long expedition to South America every year."

Holmes nodded, and then became silent for a time. I gazed into the pool at our feet and saw amid the tangle of weeds and the murky water a small golden fish swim by. Suddenly it made a dart forwards and opened its mouth as it lunged at some prey invisible to me. I caught a glimpse of long vicious teeth and realised I was looking at the famed piranha fish.

Uneasily I looked around us and noticed for the first time a glistening, corpse-coloured thing like an enormous flaccid earthworm, hanging within a bush, half-concealed by the leaves. This must be one of the leeches that had taken Anderson's life. Looking more closely I saw two more of the filthy creatures a little further away. I shuddered, and thought the whole place was filled with hungry menace.

With Doggett's help we now explored the whole inside perimeter of the terrarium. Fortunately, a narrow space was kept clear along the length of the walls to facilitate maintenance of the structure. Holmes checked especially closely the points where the stream entered and exited, but it was obvious even to me that they were too narrow, and in any case the surrounding soil showed no signs of disturbance, which it surely would have done if a man had forced his way in or out.

We went back to the entrance area, and again Holmes checked the floor carefully. He lifted his eyebrows at one point and reaching into a dark corner brought out the corpse of a small frog. It was one of the ones with black and yellow stripes I had noticed earlier. "What is this?" he asked, showing the thing to Doggett.

"*Rana palmipes*," replied Doggett promptly. "The Amazon River Frog: very common in the Amazon basin. They breed well in these conditions and provide food for the snakes and larger animals."

"I see," murmured Holmes. "But what would this particular corpse be doing so far from the foliage?"

Doggett looked a little taken aback. "I really couldn't say sir. Perhaps it was sick and crawled away to die."

"That is no doubt the explanation," said my friend, tossing the little body into the undergrowth.

"I trust," he continued, "that there will be no objection to my taking a few of the leeches for examination?"

"I'm sure there would be no objection, sir. Mrs. Anderson has already told me she intends to demolish the terrarium and I would expect the specimens to be destroyed. A great pity: it will be the end of a noble experiment. Let me get you a sack to transport them."

He left us for a short while and returned with a small coconut-fibre bag. He led the way back to the water and deftly stuffed the bag with pond weed. "There you are, sir, they should stay alive in that for at least a day, so long as you keep the weed wet."

Holmes thanked him for his trouble and together we picked a half-dozen or so of the nearest specimens from the surrounding vegetation.

We returned to the house to take our leave of Mrs. Anderson. We found her in the company of a young man of swarthy appearance. He rose and bowed, smiling, showing large and very white teeth. Mrs. Anderson also rose. "Gentlemen," she said, "may I introduce Señor Fernando Gomez, who is attached to the Brazilian embassy, and is also a friend of the family."

"I am honoured to meet you, Señor Gomez," said Holmes affably. "Can I take it you shared Mr. Anderson's interest in botany?"

Gomez smiled deprecatingly. "Ah no, sir, I am merely a diplomat and have no talent for matters of science. I am the commercial attaché for my embassy. My main concern is trade between our two great nations. There are many opportunities for exchanging our hardwoods and other natural produce for your English manufactures and it is those things that I try to encourage by making introductions, arranging translations and so on. Today however, I am here at the command of His Excellency the Ambassador to convey his personal sorrow and condolences to Mrs. Anderson."

We exchanged further conventional remarks and thanks to Mrs. Anderson for her assistance, then began the walk back to the station.

"Well, Holmes, what do you make of it?" I asked as soon as we were safely away.

"I make nothing of it so far, Watson. It is certainly a fascinating case but so far I am totally without the background to make any progress. I feel my knowledge of Brazil is sadly deficient, and I must spend some time with my books."

We took the train back and returned to Baker Street with few words exchanged. Holmes was not good company that evening, but I was content to smoke my pipe and watch him as he pulled down book after book from his shelves; blue-books, reference works, maps and so on. Some he skimmed; some he spent time perusing. Always he made copious notes. When I retired that night he was still deep in his researches.

When I awoke the next day, Sherlock Holmes was absent. I breakfasted alone and waited for news. A little before noon a boy brought a message asking me to meet Holmes at St Bartholomew's Hospital. On my arrival I went immediately to the laboratories where he carried out many of his researches. I was horrified to see him seated on a low stool, stripped to the waist. On his bare arm were fastened several small leeches, already becoming empurpled with his blood. Beside him was a basin of water, with more of the disgusting creatures swimming in it, including two of the specimens that Holmes had collected.

"You are carrying out research into the behaviour of leeches, I take it?" I said.

"Yes indeed, Watson," replied Holmes. "Here we have the European medicinal leech – *hirudo medicinalis* – vastly different in size from its Amazonian cousin of course, which can grow to a full eighteen inches in length, but in all essential features the same creature. I have been observing its method of attack. It first attaches its large tail-end sucker, then it twists its body and applies the sucker on its head to the skin, then finally it makes an incision with its teeth and feeds. When it is satiated with blood, which takes about twenty minutes with the European leech and perhaps forty minutes with the Amazonian leech, it falls off.

"Inspecting the incisions and the creatures' mouthparts under a magnifying glass, I find that they have three jaws set with many small teeth, which make a characteristic wound in the shape of the letter Y.

"It seems that in its saliva are substances to dull sensation, to dilate the victim's blood vessels to increase the flow, and to prevent the blood from clotting. Truly a remarkable creature!"

"It is certainly good at what it does," I commented dryly. "I know older doctors who have in the past used phlebotomy to treat kidney and liver disorders, but the theory of humours is quite exploded now."

"I shall be sending the results of my researches to Dr. Cronin, who is conducting the post mortem on John Anderson," explained Holmes. "I hope that he will then be able to say with some certainty which of the wounds on the body are from the leeches' activities.

"Also I have verified an important point by attaching leeches to some of the subjects. The leeches will not, or perhaps cannot, feed on the dead. It is therefore certain the Anderson was alive for some time – given the state of engorgement perhaps as much as an hour. This in itself rules out any theory of a heart attack or sudden death by another cause."

I waited while Holmes applied salve and plasters to his cuts. "If you are free, Watson, you might care to join me for lunch in Soho. I have found that there is a group of people who occasionally meet in a restaurant there that you might be interested to meet."

We took a cab to Wardour Street and Holmes guided the driver to a small and rather seedy looking restaurant. It was dark inside, and furnished with the heaviest of mahogany tables and chairs. The proprietor was obviously expecting Holmes and led us to the only occupied table. As we approached two men of foreign appearance stood up and bowed to us. Holmes made the introductions; Pedro Funari was a tall and thin man of woebegone aspect; his companion, Antonio de Moura was of average height and inclined to be stout. Both had dark complexions and beards too strong for close shaving.

"Mr. Holmes and Dr. Watson," said de Moura. "Thank you for coming."

"Gentlemen," said Sherlock Holmes, "it is you that oblige me by taking me into your confidence. I hope that we will be able to exchange information to our mutual advantage. May I introduce my friend and confidante Dr. Watson. Watson, these gentlemen are of the Brazilian Royalist party in exile."

I bowed and we all seated ourselves at the table. "Let us fortify ourselves with food before we speak of our business," said Holmes. "I am looking forward to trying the delicacies of your native land."

These came and were palatable enough, some of the dishes perhaps a little highly spiced for the average British taste, but with my experience of the cuisine of the subcontinent, I found them quite acceptable. We drank a Portuguese wine with the meal.

After the meal the proprietor brought us long, thin black cigars of a very pungent tobacco. As we relaxed over the brandy, de Moura outlined the purpose of the cabal.

"We are loyal to his majesty Dom Pedro, the rightful ruler of Brazil. In 1889 he was forced to abdicate by the army. The church was also against him because he took action against some corrupt bishops who were living at the expense of the poor. John Anderson supported the king's actions. He had met and become a friend of his Majesty some years before and was one of the people who had drawn the attention of the king to the sufferings of the people.

"After the king was overthrown, Anderson became part of our movement. His journeys to Brazil took him through the port of Belem at the mouth of the Amazon, and to Manaos where he had relatives by marriage. There he would meet with friends of the king. He took messages, money and some essential supplies back and forth. We fear he was discovered and murdered by an assassin sent by the army."

"Have you any knowledge of how he might have been betrayed?" asked Holmes.

De Moura shook his head sadly. "I do not know, sir. I cannot believe it was one of our company, who are all faithful to the death. Perhaps he made a slip or one of his messages was intercepted. I can only guess."

We stayed some time at the restaurant, Holmes asking questions and taking notes of what they would tell him of Anderson's movements. This was not much: although they did not say so, it was clear they wanted to reveal as few details as possible. Most probably they were right: the Brazilian government would have had no hesitation in executing or imprisoning those working against their state.

Finally we left, Holmes promising to send information on any developments in the case via the proprietor.

"What is perhaps most interesting Watson," said Sherlock Holmes as we walked through Soho back to our lodgings, "is that Mrs. Anderson must have known of this. Such comings and goings on such a scale could never have passed unnoticed by a spouse, and yet she claimed that her husband had no strong political opinions."

"Perhaps she was protecting his name?" I ventured.

"To what purpose at this juncture? He is dead and no Englishman would think the worse of him for helping those of another country gain their freedom. No, she wished to conceal the matter from us for some reason, and that reason is undoubtedly concerned with the manner of his death, rather than the fact of it."

A few days later, I received another summons from Sherlock Holmes. I found him poring over a lengthy document. "The results of the post mortem, Watson," he announced. "Dr. Cronin has kindly sent me the details in advance of their formal presentation at the inquest. The immediate cause of cause of death was loss of blood. There were also some respiratory problems, as the blood was deoxygenated. Post mortem finds no signs of heart disease or a stroke. Yet lesions on the face acquired before death show that he was not able to stop himself falling, as if he were smitten by a sudden paralysis."

"That is not typical of a malaria faint," I commented. "Normally the victim would feel sick and dizzy and sit or lie down before the fever made him collapse."

Holmes read on. "The minor injuries are all listed: apart from the facial injuries there were some scratches on the hand; some recent bruising on the hip and a small puncture in the sole of the left foot." He put the papers aside and slouched into his chair, puffing at his pipe. After some time he spoke.

"I believe we must return to the scene, Watson. I sorely need to make further investigations that I carelessly omitted last time."

Once more we took the train to Kew Gardens station. After making our bows to Mrs. Anderson, who did not seem best pleased at seeing us again, we were passed on to Doggett and conducted to the terrarium. After we had been left alone, Holmes dropped into a crouch and searched the floor near the entrance, paying especial care to the area around the bench. At last he gave an exclamation. "Here we are, Watson! – as I expected." He reached very carefully behind the bench and drew up between the tips of two fingers a small tangled object. Holmes held it well away from me, but I could see it was a clump of two long and twisted thorns.

"They look vicious, certainly," I said doubtfully. "They may well be from the plants we have seen deeper into the foliage here."

"Undoubtedly, but observe the tips! Carefully, for your life!"

I looked more closely and saw that there appeared to be dark matter on the points. "You suspect poison?" I asked.

"A poison, Watson, which causes loss of muscular control, but not death. Coupled with the scene of the Amazonian jungle, does that convey nothing to you?"

"Curare!"

"Exactly: curare. Discovered centuries ago by the native indians of South America. It is prepared by boiling the bark of a certain vine for days until it is reduced to a resinous dark mass containing large proportions of the plant-poison. As it takes effect only through a cut, it is admirably suited for smearing on to arrowheads, or as in this case, a thorn. The dosage is important and varies with the size of the victim: a bird will die in under a minute, a small mammal in ten minutes and a large creature such as a man in perhaps twenty minutes. You will recall the dead frog I found, Watson. It is a common indian trick to test the potency by pricking a frog with a poisoned dart then counting the number of hops it is able to make before succumbing. I believe the frog was a victim of such a test.

"Observe also how the clump is rather crushed in appearance. It was placed in one of Anderson's working boots. When he stood up, he drove the thorn deep into his foot, accounting for the small puncture observed by Dr. Cronin. No doubt he cursed, but thought it had simply dropped into the boot on a previous visit. He extracted and discarded it as we have seen. A few minutes later, by which time he had reached the pool, paralysis would have overtaken him and he fell: a helpless prey to the leeches. The poison would be undetectable – current medical science has no test sensitive enough to detect a dose of curare that is not fatal."

I considered this for a short time, and came to an obvious conclusion. "Can I take it you suspect Mrs. Anderson of the deed?" I asked my friend.

"I certainly suspect her of the execution of the murder. Only she or Doggett could reasonably have come to this place without question, or know his habits so well as to set the trap. I am less certain that hers was the will behind it.

The thought of curare as a means of execution would most naturally occur to one of indian descent. I am inclined to think that Señor Gomez was the guiding mind and provided the means. My study of physiology leads me to believe that he is part indian."

"But why would she agree to such a thing?"

"Why else but for love, Watson?" asked my friend with the sneer he habitually used when mentioning the softer passions. "Why does a woman do anything but for love? It is clear that her tenderness for Anderson has faded over the years. She told us herself that she still feels this to be an alien land, and longs constantly for the warmth and companionship of her native country. There are no children to tie her here and perhaps bond the marriage. Anderson had his hobby and was often away for months at a time without her. Also, he is far older than her.

"Then one day a young man from her own country pays a visit. He talks to her in her own language of the scenes of her homeland. After perhaps a short time she falls in love with him. They exchange confidences as lovers do and she reveals that Anderson is a spy for the royalist cause. As a good diplomat he reports this to his superiors and receives the order to kill him."

"But even so," I protested, "it is one thing to elope with a lover, and quite another to commit murder at his behest. She would be left in a very precarious position in many ways."

"You are quite correct, Watson, and therefore I believe he offered her a powerful inducement: marriage and a new life in the country she loves."

"Would he go as far as marriage merely to advance his career?"

Holmes shrugged. "From his point of view it would be an advantageous match. She is after all the daughter of a senior government official, and of course she inherits all Anderson's wealth, which is not inconsiderable here, and would be counted a fortune in Brazil. All in all, an excellent match for one of his descent."

"But the manner of the death, Holmes! The horror of curare poisoning is that the victim is awake and aware of what is happening until the loss of consciousness. He would have felt the leeches feeding on him, but have been unable to call out or even gesture!"

"Indeed," said Holmes. "A most unpleasant end. Come, I believe it is time we had a conversation with Mrs. Anderson."

We returned to the house and requested a private conversation of its lady.

Without preamble Holmes enquired, "I understand, Mrs. Anderson, that you are affianced to Señor Gomez?"

The woman became rigid with surprise and shock, which was of course Holmes' intention, to throw her off balance and perhaps to make her say more than she intended.

"How could you know that?" she demanded. "We have told no-one!"

Holmes made an easy gesture. "The process of deduction, Madame, just as I have deduced that you killed your husband through the use of curare."

Again she stiffened with shock, and perhaps fear. For a moment I thought she was about to faint. Instead, she staggered to a chair and sat down, her mouth working silently. In a few seconds she had regained some control of herself.

"I trust you have not mentioned this ridiculous theory to the police?" she inquired with an attempt at hauteur.

Holmes' expression was unforgiving. "Not yet madam, but I have collected evidence which I believe would convince them of your guilt. I can feel little sympathy for you, Mrs. Anderson. It was after all a cold-blooded killing. Am I right in thinking it was inspired by Señor Gomez?"

She straightened her head in proud defiance. "I will not put the blame for my deed upon another. It was my hand that placed the thorns. I had lost my love for my husband, and he was a traitor to my country. I wished to be free. Fernando merely provided me with the means."

"Well, as a foreign diplomat he may not be arraigned, and I cannot let you hang, and him go free. But I can insist madam that you both leave this country by the next boat, otherwise I will tell the police all I know."

She bowed her head in acquiescence.

We left immediately, Holmes' brow as black as thunder. "A dirty business, Watson," he exclaimed. "One of the most cold-blooded killings I have ever seen, and yet we cannot bring the perpetrators to justice. Our only consolation is that I cannot believe such a pair will have joy of each other.

"I will make my report to Sir Joseph. He should know the full facts, although I have no doubt that he will agree that we need not interfere with any conclusions the coroner may draw. But as for anything else, you will have to keep your counsel."

"  have an interesting letter here, Watson" said my friend Sherlock Holmes one morning. Mrs. Hudson had just brought up the post and Holmes was languidly sorting the wheat of commissions from the chaff of bills and idle correspondence.

"A case?" I asked.

"Yes, if I decide to take it. The client lives in Birmingham which will interrupt the even tenor of my life – and yours if you decide to accompany me – but then again I am becoming a little stale in the metropolis and a change of scene in a strange town may be exactly what I need."

He passed the letter over to me and I read as follows:

'SIR –

While the intrusion of outsiders into what are purely family matters is deeply distasteful to me, nevertheless I believe your skill in detecting impostors and charlatans may be valuable.

I would ask you to present yourself at my offices on the 21st of this month, when I will give you full details. You will find your remuneration paid at the most generous scale.

Yours faithfully,

JAMES MURCHISON'

I studied the letterhead, which was that of Murchison's Haberdashery, which I knew to be a large manufacturing concern.

"Mr. Murchison is rather peremptory in his tone," I remarked.

"Indeed," said my friend, "but I am inclined to be charitable and to attribute at least some of that to concern

73

for his family. You will have noted how the pen has dug deeper at the words 'impostors' and 'charlatans'. There is also the matter of my finances, which could certainly stand help from a rich and grateful client. Yes, Watson, on consideration I believe I will go to Birmingham and I hope that you will accompany me."

The date Murchison had specified was only two days hence. A little time was spent in sending a telegram confirming the appointment and in consulting Bradshaw, and more in packing our bags for a visit of a few days, but the next day saw us getting into a first-class smoker at Euston.

A journey of somewhat more than two hours took us to Birmingham New Street station, from where we were able to hire a hansom cab to the premises of Murchison Haberdashery. It was a remarkable building, being four stories high with each storey in a different architectural style and with a large square tower at each corner. We gave our names to the porter and a boy showed us the way to Murchison's office, which was located in one of the towers. We entered a spacious and palatial room with fine marble on the walls and floor. Mr. Murchison rose to greet us. He was a large and imposing person; clearly a self-made man of great force.

"Ah, Mr. Holmes, I am delighted to meet you," he said. "And you too, of course, Dr. Watson." We both bowed. "If you will be seated, I will outline the problem."

We all seated ourselves. Murchison seemed uncharacteristically hesitant for a man of his character. Finally, he decided how to open the matter. "I wish you, Mr. Holmes, to expose a fraudster." He hesitated again. "Of a rather unusual kind."

"Such a task would be both a duty and a pleasure," murmured Holmes, clearly trying to put the man at ease. "Please give us the full details of the affair."

"It is also, I have to say, a matter most embarrassing to me. It is essential that no word of this be generally known."

"I assure you Mr. Murchison; my discretion is absolute, as is that of Dr. Watson."

"Certainly," I interjected.

"Well then, it is not I, but my wife who is being most cruelly deceived. You should know that we lost our son – our only child – in the Transvaal war a few years ago. My wife was inconsolable, until that is just recently when she fell into the power of a woman who calls herself a medium; a Madame Beverley. This woman claims to be in touch with the spirit of our boy and relays messages from the Beyond."

He looked sharply at Holmes, "I take it Mr. Holmes you give no credence to such beliefs?"

"None, I assure you," said my friend coolly.

"Very well then. My wife is completely under the spell of this woman. She talks of nothing but the séances she attends and the messages that purportedly come from our child.

"There is also the question of money – the medium of course charges for her services and some considerable sums have been paid over. I believe the greater part of my wife's allowance for each month goes to this woman."

Holmes looked thoughtful. "There are of course certain legal restrictions on mediums. You have no doubt explored this aspect of the affair?"

"I have. I consulted my man of business, who has studied the law concerning these matters. His opinion is that as the woman is properly housed, an action cannot be brought under the Vagrancy Act, which is often used against gypsies and fortune-tellers. Essentially, unless the medium predicts misfortune it is not illegal to practice. She has been careful in fact to predict nothing at all – she claims to be merely a conduit for the voice of our son."

"I see," said my friend thoughtfully. "This is certainly an unusual case. We have a wrongdoer who is committing a fraud that is based on the supernatural. The normal rules of evidence therefore do not apply. It will be impossible to prove that something has or has not taken place. The medium can pass on messages she claims come from the spirit world and there is no-one, not the Archbishop of Canterbury nor the Pope in Rome, can say they did not."

Murchison made a gesture of acquiescence. "I know this. I was hoping that with your noted skills you might be able to see a way through."

"Well, I will see what can be done. If the medium uses some of the characteristic tricks of her trade, then it may well be possible to demonstrate a fraud to your wife. I must however tell you, that in such cases as these the victim often goes on believing in the charlatan simply because of their desperate need for comfort, and dismisses the fraud as a minor incident."

We sat in gloomy silence for a short while. Then Holmes questioned Murchison on the details of the matter; the frequency of the séances; the amount of money involved and so on. Finally, after about half an hour he drew the matter to a close. "I think that is as much as we can achieve today, Mr. Murchison. The next step is clearly to interview your wife. Can we arrange to call at your home tomorrow morning?"

Murchison tugged at his moustache. "I can understand that that is a necessary part of your investigations, but how will I explain your wish to question her?"

Holmes made an airy gesture, "That is not a problem. Dr. Watson and myself can be, let us say, members of the Psychical Research Society attached to King's College, London. There is in fact no such society but it is not likely your lady wife will check the matter. We will say that we have heard glowing reports of Madame Beverley and wish to talk to one that knows her. From that, we will ask to be introduced and to attend a séance."

Murchison nodded. "I see. That would do very well. I can also help you by having visiting cards engraved. In Birmingham, we pride ourselves on our readiness to trade and the speed of our operations and I know of a jobbing printer that can produce your cards this very afternoon."

Holmes quickly jotted down the text to be engraved on the cards, and Mr. Murchison recommended a nearly hotel which would be convenient for the centre of our investigations. We then took our leave.

We found the hotel comfortable enough, and that evening after dinner we repaired to the lounge where we made ourselves comfortable and prepared to discuss the matter. Holmes filled his churchwarden while I took my cigar.

"Allow me to outline some of the tricks used by mediums," said my friend as he pulled meditatively on his pipe. "We must be on the alert for them at the séance. Firstly, the room will be darkened; ostensibly because spirits are repelled by light, but in truth to conceal as far as possible the medium's actions. Mediums almost always work at their own homes – you will hardly ever see a peripatetic medium. The reason is not far to seek: so many things then become possible. Objects and apparatus can be concealed before the clients arrive. A collaborator can be hidden behind a screen or curtains: that person can make sounds, shine lights or even cause droplets of water to fall from the ceiling.

"The medium may also have apparatus concealed about her person. She may have hooks up her sleeves that can be shaken down and used for manipulation. She may have emery boards strapped to her legs that can be rubbed together to make eerie sounds. There are a thousand tricks, and I hope to see some ingenious variants of them in the course of these investigations."

"But surely not every single medium is fraudulent." I protested. "We must surely give credence to the very many expert observers. For example Helen Berry in America is said to have formed a small child from ectoplasm in the presence of witnesses. It made imploring motions with its hands and moved its lips although no sound was heard. Everybody found it a most moving sight. How could such a scene possibly be faked?"

Sherlock Holmes removed his pipe and gestured with it. "I might suggest gauzy fabric covered with fluorescent paint. An accomplice could lower or wave such a device and imagination would do the rest."

"But still," I persisted, "eminent scientists have carried out experiments in the strictest conditions. Mediums have had their garments changed under supervision and taken into experimental rooms to which they have had no previous access and still produced startling effects."

Holmes nodded. "Yes, I have read of some such, but I am still far from convinced. After all, if such as we can be baffled by Maskelyne and Cooke's demonstrations at the Egyptian Hall why not a scientist? I might speculate that the most convincing tests of a medium's skills would be carried out not by a man of science, but by a conjurer."

"You are convinced then that this Madame Beverley is a fraud?"

"A consulting detective would be severely handicapped if he allowed that the supernatural might be an explanation, Watson. I fear that if I attempted to tell a client that his diamond necklace had been stolen by a maleficent demon, shall we say, that he would not remain a client long. Nor would he be likely to pay me. No, I believe in the natural human drives: the strong need of a bereaved mother to be comforted and the lust for money in the wicked person who takes advantage of her."

I shook my head at my friend's obdurate rationalism and soon after retired to bed.

We took breakfast at the usual time, and shortly afterwards our mock visiting cards were delivered as had been promised. At ten o'clock we ordered a cab and rattled through the streets of Birmingham to Murchison's home in Edgbaston. We arrived at an imposing mansion, obviously built but a few years before. We gave in our cards at the door and were conducted to the drawing room where we were greeted by our client and his wife.

"Mr. Holmes; Dr. Watson," she murmured as she offered us her hand. "I am very pleased to see you. I understand you are here in connection with Madame Beverley."

"That is indeed the case, madam", said Holmes. "Remarkable stories of her powers have reached the ears of our Society and we have been despatched to look into the matter further."

"I would be more than happy to help you: Madame Beverley has given me new life and I owe her a great deal. Please be seated and I will be glad to answer your questions."

"Can you first tell me," said Sherlock Holmes, producing a notebook, "when you first made the acquaintance of this lady?"

"That would be about four months ago."

"And how did it happen that you met her?"

"She wrote to me, Mr Holmes, at this address. She told me that my son Thomas had come to her when she was in a mediumistic trance and had asked her to contact me. When I read those words I was at first shocked and disgusted beyond measure. It is common knowledge that we had a son who had been killed in the South-African campaign and I believed the letter to be a vulgar attempt to persuade me to attend her séances. But then her letter went on to say that to the last he remembered my quoting: 'Where there is fear, there cannot be wisdom' ".

" ' *Ubi timor adest, sapientia adesse nequit*', " I supplied.

"Quite right, Dr. Watson: a saying of Lactanius, an early Christian and himself a sojourner in Africa. It is one of my favourite quotations, but one we kept between us and could not have been known by anyone else. I contacted her the next day and was invited to a séance the day after." She paused, apparently overcome by the memory. "I do not know if you can believe me Mr. Holmes; certainly my husband cannot; but at that séance my son spoke to me!"

"You recognised his voice then?"

"It was somewhat changed in timbre, Mr. Holmes – it was rather hoarser than Tom used and a little slurred, but all the turns of phrase were his, and he spoke of incidents from his childhood which I had forgotten myself until he reminded me. The time for instance that he had been given a model steamship for his tenth birthday and we took it to the river

Cole to try it out. The current carried it away and Tom began to cry, but then Peters, a groom we had at that time, ran down the bank and waded out in his clothes to recover the toy."

"That certainly seems to show remarkable powers in the medium," said Holmes politely. "To pursue the matter of your son's voice, do I understand you to say that he spoke neither in Madame Beverley's voice, nor in his own?"

"That is correct. The voice is much lower than a woman could produce, but at the same time it is some way from that which Tom used in life. Madame Beverley believes that the wrench of the Great Change has made an alteration in the way we perceive his voice on this earth."

"I see. Now can we turn to your son himself. What sort of a man was he?"

Mrs. Murchison indicated a photograph in the imperial size standing on a nearby table. It showed a good-looking young man in a subaltern's uniform. "This photograph was made just before he left for the Transvaal. As you see he was a handsome and well-made man."

"He wears the uniform of the 58th Regiment of Foot," observed Holmes.

"Yes – the Rutlandshires. My family is from Oakham and we have service connections with the regiment."

"The 58th is one of our hardiest regiments," interposed Mr. Murchison proudly. "The men are nick-named the Steel-Backs because of their complete indifference to floggings." I noticed that Mrs. Murchison winced slightly at this.

"He was always a romantic, Mr. Holmes," continued Mrs. Murchison. "He was much influenced by the glory of Empire and the poetry of Mrs. Hemans. He insisted on joining the regiment, and we did not oppose him."

"Indeed not," said Mr. Murchison. "We were glad to see him do his duty for Queen and country. It was also, I believed, advantageous for him to find an outlet for his youthful energy; to see the world and to lead men. In a few years of course, I would have hoped that he would come back to England and settle down to learning the business, and eventually take over the running of it from me."

"Sadly, however, this was not to be," continued Mrs. Murchison. "He was sent with his regiment to put down the Transvaal rebellion and killed in action at the battle of Majuba Hill."

"That battle was about three years ago, I believe?" asked Holmes.

"That is correct."

"And have you had any further information regarding his death?"

"I have some knowledge: the enemy did not keep to fixed lines, but advanced under cover and shot very accurately at our forces. The order was given to retreat, but the Boers having attained the summit the retreat turned into a rout. In that confusion my Thomas was shot in the head and died instantly."

"Was it Madame Beverley that described the battle thus?" asked my friend.

"Thomas speaking through Madame Beverley," corrected Mrs. Murchison with a gentle smile.

"Of course," said Holmes. "A very circumstantial account which has the stamp of veracity." He jotted a little in his notebook, then closed it and said: "I believe your very kind assistance has given us all me need for the moment. The next step of course would be to attend a séance and afterwards talk to Madame Beverley. Might I ask if we could rely on your good offices to arrange such a meeting?"

"Would this evening be convenient?"

"Eminently so. But are you sure that she will be free at such short notice?"

"Certainly. I am after all her only client."

"Indeed. That is quite unusual. Do you know why she has not held sittings for other bereaved persons?"

"She has explained that it is an enormous effort to reach beyond the veil, and she is not physically a strong woman. I give her enough to live on – it is after all a comparatively small sum – and the arrangement suits us both. Let me write down her address from you. It is in the district of Handsworth, not far from the centre of town. Madame Beverley normally sits at 8 o'clock, so perhaps you could arrive for half-past seven."

We took our leave of the couple with appropriate words and as we walked down the drive together Holmes shared his thoughts with me.

"There is no question that someone who knew Thomas Murchison well is involved here," he observed. "I might speculate it is a servant of long standing, perhaps still in employment with the family. Such a person would be familiar with Thomas's history and his manner of speech. We can deduce further that this person has himself been in military service – the description of the manner and order of the battle is well beyond a civilian's knowledge. This narrows the field still more.

"If we can find that person we have to a large extent solved the case. We can cut off the flow of revelations at source. We then need only concern ourselves with Madame Beverley's methods."

That evening we sallied from our hotel and hired a hansom to take us to Handsworth, which we found to be a respectable working-class neighbourhood. As we paid off the cabman, a wild-looking fellow accosted us. He was dressed in clean but shabby blacks, but what was most striking to me were his very large and protuberant eyes. He looked intently from one of our faces to the other.

"Are you about to visit the woman that speaks with the dead?" he inquired in a low but passionate voice.

Holmes took it upon himself to answer the man. "We are. What can you tell us about her?"

"I can tell you that your immortal souls are in danger! Does it not say in the book of Deuteronomy: 'There shall not be found among you any one that maketh his son or his daughter to pass through the fire, or that useth divination, or an observer of times, or an enchanter, or a witch, or a charmer, or a consulter with familiar spirits, or a wizard, or a necromancer. For all that do these things are an abomination unto the Lord: and because of these abominations the Lord thy God doth drive them out from before thee.' "

"But all this to the side," persisted Sherlock Holmes, "what can you tell us of Madame Beverley?"

The man looked at him incredulously. "She is a witch! What more do you need to know? Do not enter her presence! She is beautiful, no doubt, but so is any succubus or lamia that would entrap a man. 'Thou shalt not suffer a witch to live!' – Exodus twenty-two eighteen."

"The law frowns on such action in our times," murmured Holmes.

"To our ultimate ruin! Do we not learn from the Witch of Endor? Did not King Saul grievously sin by commanding the witch to raise the ghost of the prophet Samuel and was thereupon overthrown and killed?"

No doubt concluding that the man had nothing of substance to tell us, my friend merely smiled and turned away.

We climbed the steps to the entrance and rang the bell. The door was opened by a small, rather rotund lady in a purple dress and a state of high excitement. "Good evening, good evening!" she exclaimed. "Mr. Holmes and Dr. Watson, I presume – the investigators from King's College? Mrs. Murchison told us you would be coming. Such a dear lady! I give thanks nightly that Madame Beverley has been able to bring her comfort. Madame Beverley is in excellent form tonight – I'm sure we won't be disappointed! I am Mrs. Barnard, the next-door neighbour. I've always been interested in the spirit world and I'm so grateful that Madame Beverley allows me to assist at her evenings!"

Still chattering she led us a few steps down the hall and into a small parlour. The space in the room was largely taken up by a large, circular mahogany table. A number of dining chairs were placed about the table, and also a larger chair with arms and wings. Mrs. Murchison was already present and talking to a slightly-built and pretty young woman. At our entrance the young lady came over to greet us and we were able to make use once more of our false visiting cards. "Mr. Holmes, Dr. Watson," she said in a composed manner. "Welcome to my home."

"Thank you madam," said Holmes, "we are most grateful that we may be present to witness the work of one who is in such close touch with the Great Beyond."

She inclined her head and smiled charmingly. "You are very kind. May I ask if the work of your society progresses well?"

"It does," said Holmes smoothly, "although sadly there are still many who will not open their minds to the infinite."

"There they show their narrowness of thought," returned the young woman. "As the Bard says, 'there are more things in heaven and earth, Horatio, than are dreamt of in your philosophy.' "

I entered a question here in my role as secretary. "May I ask for our report: is it Miss or Mrs. Beverley?"

"I prefer Madame," she said with a smile.

"Of course," I said, making a note.

After a little more conversation, the arrangements were made for the séance. Mrs. Barnard bustled about, extinguishing most lights and turning down others. Holmes asked if I could sit near one of the lights as I would be taking notes, which was granted. The final arrangement was that the medium took her place in the large, winged chair, with Holmes and Mrs. Murchison on either side of her, and Mrs. Barnard and I placed beyond them.

While settling myself, I dropped my pencil. I scrambled under the table for it for a few moments and reappeared muttering my apologies.

The medium leaned back in her chair with her eyes closed. She moved her head about at random, "Thomas!" she called in a commanding voice. "Thomas! Your mother is here!" Nothing changed. The medium again rocked in her chair and again called on the dead man. This was repeated several times. Abruptly, her face went slack. Her head lolled against one wing of the chair. Her breathing became stertorous.

'HER HEAD LOLLED AGAINST ONE WING OF THE CHAIR'

Her mouth opened and a voice came from it – but not her own: it was much lower and hoarser in tone and seemed somehow hollow. "Mother!" it said.

"Tom!" cried Mrs. Murchison wildly. "I'm here!"

"Mother, you must not grieve," said the voice. "I have gone where we all must go, and only a few years before. Soon enough we will be together."

"Oh, Tom, I miss you so much!" wailed the bereaved woman.

"I cannot stay. I am called. Be happy, mother."

"Oh, not so soon, Tom: please stay!"

"I cannot this time. Perhaps next time. Please come again to speak to me."

"I will! I will!" sobbed Mrs. Murchison.

There was silence for a time, then the medium stirred. Abruptly, she came to herself, and looked about in some apparent confusion. "Did it work?" she asked, "was Thomas here?"

"Indeed he was, Madame Beverley," said Mrs. Murchison. "You are always so reliable a channel. He could only stay a very short time, but he had comforting words for me as always."

"I'm so glad," murmured the medium, "but now dear Mrs. Murchison; gentlemen; may I ask you to leave me? My apologies for this rudeness, but I am so weary after séances. Forgive me; but I cannot stand to see you out."

We sprang to our feet at once. "There is no need to apologise after such exertions as you have undergone, madam," said Holmes. "I believe we have enough for our report and we are most grateful to you. I will speak to our Secretary on our return and hope that he will be able to remit a suitable fee for your kindness."

"As you wish, Mr. Holmes; my needs are few. As the Poet has said, 'he is well paid that is well satisfied.'"

"Let me show your visitors out and then make you a cup of tea!" exclaimed Mrs. Barnard. The medium gave her a grateful smile.

We left together. Mrs. Murchison offered us a lift in her brougham but Holmes declined this and we said our farewells for the evening.

"I have to say, Holmes," I remarked, "that Madame Beverley struck me as a most sincere and open young woman."

Sherlock Holmes smiled in a cynical manner. "The highest praise that one can give to an actor, Watson, is that he has convincingly imitated sincerity."

"We have no evidence that she was an actress!"

"On the contrary; it is quite obvious. You noted of course, the quotations from *Hamlet* and *The Merchant of Venice*. The former is often misquoted, but she gave it accurately. Also she wears cosmetics, which have been expertly applied, but applied rather in the manner used in the acting profession – that is, rather bold strokes and more emphatic colouring so that the effect is best seen from beyond the footlights. Another point – although perhaps here I stretch the matter – the name 'Beverley' may be from Sheridan's *The Rivals*, where Jack Absolute takes that name when he wishes to conceal his identity."

"I see," I muttered, taken somewhat aback.

"I wonder if there is a man behind the affair? I observed no traces of a male presence and she was unclear about her marital state. In English society 'Madame' may be taken as a courtesy title for a married or unmarried woman."

I coughed, "Well in fact, Holmes, there is one thing I noticed and that is that the lady is in an interesting condition."

Holmes raised his eyebrows, "Indeed?" he said.

"Yes, I am quite certain. I noticed the raised colour in her cheeks and the slight thickening of her waist as we were introduced. I dropped my pencil deliberately so as to be able to get a glimpse of her ankles – they were slightly swollen: the typical oedema of pregnancy. I would say she was in her fourth or fifth month."

"My word, Doctor," laughed my friend, "you have certainly trumped me there! I noted of course that her dress was a little tight at the bosom and waist, but attributed it to a recent gain in weight with the better living she is making at present."

I felt absurdly pleased at this praise from the master of deduction.

"So through your acute observation," he continued, "we are now aware that there is a man in the picture, but she is not anxious that the fact be known. This of course immediately raises the question 'Why not?' There is no reason why a medium should not have a husband, and many do."

I noticed that we were not retracing our steps towards our hotel. "Where are we bound?" I asked.

"I was not idle this afternoon, Watson. In fact I have been able to put a little work the way of a local tradesman. Come with me and we will see if he has completed my task."

"Is it not rather late?"

"Not at all: as Mr. Murchison has already informed us, in Birmingham they are happy to work long hours to oblige a client."

Holmes led me through some narrow and dirty streets to a yard above which was the sign: 'Jas. Ellis – File & Rasp Manufacturer'. Holmes led the way to an old and peeling door and knocked on it. It was opened by an unshaven and disreputable individual – presumably Ellis himself. He leered in an offensive manner on seeing Holmes.

"'Evening, governor," he said familiarly. "I've got your job here. That'll be two sovereigns, as we agreed." With those words he handed over a small parcel done up in brown paper.

It seemed a large sum for a job that could not possibly have taken more than a few hours, but Holmes paid up on the spot. As we left, Ellis was leaning on his door frame and looking after us, still wearing a knowing smirk that I could not decipher.

We summoned a cab and retired to our hotel. "Get a few hours rest, Watson, then we must pay a return visit to Madame Beverley!" he said breezily. I raised my eyebrows at this: he could only mean that we were to break into the house, but I made no protest.

In the early hours of the morning Holmes tapped on my door. I came out of a light doze immediately, gripped by the excitement of the chase. I had only removed my outer clothing, so was ready to accompany him in a very short time. We left the hotel by the back door, Holmes carrying his Gladstone bag.

There was no question of getting a cab at that hour, so we walked for somewhat over a mile back to Handsworth. Turning into Madame Beverley's road we took care to proceed quietly so as not to awaken any light sleepers. Outside the house, Holmes gave a casual glance around to ensure that we were unobserved, then led the way down the steps to the area. There he opened his Gladstone bag and produced the parcel he had been given by Ellis. Unwrapping it he disclosed a curiously-shaped apparatus. It was a slim steel rod mounted on a stout wooden handle. The end of the rod had been beaten flat and curved into a hook. Holmes pushed the rod between the leaves of the sash and felt around carefully, peering at the sash lock as he did so. When it was in a position to suit him, he gave the handle a strong twist which caused the hook to force the lock open. We raised the sash carefully and climbed into the room. Holmes quietly lowered and latched the window again.

From his bag Holmes now produced a dark lantern, lit it and shone it around the room. It seemed to be a general workroom. I saw pieces of sewing and other domestic paraphernalia. Holmes shone the light upwards and we saw a rubber tube, several feet in length and perhaps two inches in diameter, protruding from a circular hole in the plaster of the ceiling. I recognised it as a speaking tube of the type that is often used by householders to interrogate callers without opening the door.

"There you have it, Watson," murmured my friend. "The accomplice is stationed by that tube. It runs up inside the medium's chair and terminates in one of the chair wings. By putting it to his ear he can clearly hear what is happening at the séance, and at the proper times he can speak into the tube. His voice then appears to emanate from the medium's mouth. A simple but effective trick."

We searched the room for papers or belongings that might shed further light on the person who spoke into the tube, but found nothing with a name on it, although there were ample signs of male occupancy. We obviously could not go to the upper floors as the risk of detection would be too great. Finally we put everything back where we had found it and left the house by the area door. Holmes used a sheet of card to ensure that the spring lock did not make a sound.

"Well at least we have proof that she is a fraud," I said hopefully as we walked back through the empty streets. "We can easily insist on showing the apparatus to Mrs. Murchison."

"I am not yet satisfied, Watson. Certainly we can expose the basis of the fraud and it is very likely – although as I said at the start of this case not inevitable – that this will be enough to destroy Mrs. Murchison's belief in this medium. However, we will not have got to the heart of the problem. Somewhere, there is a person with an intimate knowledge of Tom's life who is prepared to betray his memory for money. I owe it to my client to find that person and expose him."

Sherlock Holmes was normally an early riser, but having had so few hours of sleep the night before, he was still in bed at nine o'clock. For myself, having always been irregular in the hours I keep, I found myself wakeful at that hour. After taking breakfast, it occurred to me to do a little investigation on my own account.

I was aware that old soldiers, like others with a common interest or common experiences, would typically meet in certain public-houses to talk and exchange reminiscences with their fellows. It occurred to me that, given Holmes' deduction that the informer was a former military man, he might well find it convenient and congenial to drink in whatever public-house was used by the old soldiers of

Handsworth. I decided to make it my business to find this hostelry and ask a few questions of the landlord and customers. I flattered myself that mention of my time of attachment to the Fifth Northumberland Fusiliers would encourage the men to speak easily to me, and hoped I would be able to work the conversation round to the South Africa campaign.

Leaving a note for Holmes, I took myself off on my task. A few hours later I was back at our hotel and burst intemperately into my friend's room, where I found him relaxing with the *Daily Telegraph*. "Holmes, I have solved the case!" I exclaimed triumphantly.

Sherlock Holmes smiled and leaned back in his chair. "Well done, Watson! The pupil at last excels the master!" he exclaimed. "May I now, as the tables are turned, beg you to explain your reasoning to me?" I detected more than a hint of chaffing in his tone, but was confident I would persuade him I was in the right.

"I have found a public-house in Handsworth where old soldiers meet," I explained. "It is called the *Black Eagle*. I went there this morning and talked to the landlord and I was told that one of his regulars was injured at Majuba Hill! Your theory that a servant of the Murchisons is involved is mistaken. It is clear that this man must have been a comrade of young Tom Murchison. In the long periods of boredom between marches they would have exchanged all sorts of confidences. He would have found all the small details of Tom's life: fondly remembered incidents from childhood; the names of his uncles and aunts and so on. Also of course he would have noted his manner of speaking and turns of phrase.

"After being discharged as wounded, he returned to his native town. There he takes up with the woman we know as Madame Beverley and between them they hit on the perfect way of making money. Together with his accomplice or leman he would purport to be in contact with the spirit of the dead. He cannot imitate Tom's voice so he simply speaks hoarsely. This also explains," I continued, anxious not to leave any loose ends, "why she conceals the man's existence. If we spoke to him we would recognise his voice and perhaps the injury would give away his military background. Let us give the matter to the police and have the pair arrested."

Holmes pondered the matter. "This young man, the fraudster, do you know the nature of his injuries?"

I was puzzled by this question. "He was hit by a rifle bullet in the jaw, I understand, Holmes, but what has that to do with the case?"

"Well it may have significance – can you not see how?"

Sherlock Holmes rose to his feet. "You have provided the missing piece of the puzzle, Watson. We will certainly pay a visit to Madame Beverley and her accomplice. The police I think will be unnecessary."

A short while later we knocked on the medium's door. She opened it herself, and looked surprised and wary as she saw us standing there.

"Good afternoon, madam," said Holmes, making a bow. "I wonder if it would be convenient for myself and Dr. Watson to have a word with you?"

"As you wish," she said. She was clearly not overjoyed to see us, but nevertheless stepped aside to allow us to enter and gestured us into the parlour where we had previously held the séance. The room looked shabbier in the daylight than it had done with the curtains drawn and the gas lit. The rugs and furniture were well worn, and had obviously not been of particularly good quality to begin with.

Madame Beverley shut the door and joined us. She did not invite us to be seated, and remained standing herself. "And what can I do for you, Mr. Holmes?" she asked.

"Before I begin, may I ask that your gentleman companion join us? What I have to say concerns him as much as yourself."

She stared at him, clearly considering what response to make. "I conduct all the business in this house, Mr. Sherlock

Holmes," she said at last in a frosty tone. "You may state your concerns."

"Very well. I wish to appeal to you as a woman who is shortly to become a mother herself, to consider the feelings of another mother who has lost her child."

"I fail to understand you."

"Mrs. Murchison grieves for her lost son. She lives her life under a pall because of it and a day does not pass without her feeling the pain of it. You are aware that on the contrary Thomas Murchison is very much alive. I am here to ask you both to make a confession to his parents. I may tell you frankly that if you do not, then I shall."

Madame Beverley said nothing but stood stricken by a mixture of emotions I could only guess at. At that moment, we heard footsteps ascending the stairs from the basement. The door opened and a young man walked in. The lower part of his face was muffled in a scarf.

"I was listening at the speaking tube," he explained. He took Madame Beverley's hand and led her to the sofa and made her sit. "Please be seated gentlemen," he said to us.

We took our seats on the dining chairs and after a pause to collect his thoughts the young man told us his story. I had to strain somewhat to hear it, for his voice had a severe slur to it and the scarf deadened the sound.

"You are correct, gentlemen, in deducing that I am Thomas Murchison," he began.

"From the moment we landed in Africa we were fighting an enemy we did not know how to deal with. The Boers did not stand to battle in the way we were used to: they were all excellent shots with their rifles and shot at us from cover. We suffered a continuous loss of men. Also, they were dressed in their ordinary farming clothes – often in browns or other earth colours; they were almost invisible against that arid landscape. We of course wore our regimentals: scarlet coats, blue trousers and white helmets.

"We were marched into the Drakensberg mountains and there came a time when it was ordered that we encamp on

Majuba Hill. About six hundred of us were present from several regiments, including the Rutlandshires. The top of the hill is a large shallow basin in which we set up our camp. The Boers attacked us later that day: they fired their rifles from behind boulders and were very accurate. To return fire our men had to stand on the perimeter ridge where they were exposed. They were killed one by one. Finally the picquets fell back into the centre but that allowed the Boers to gain the ridge and fire down into the mass of us in the basin. You could barely see the enemy, gentlemen; the smoke from their rapidly-firing rifles was so thick.

"We attempted a retreat down the hill, but in truth it was more that we ran for our lives than retreated. In the scramble I was wounded in the face, the bullet entering behind my left ear and shattering my jaw as it exited. I rolled the rest of the way down the slope and lay unconscious for a time. When I came to myself it was almost dark. I crawled away: I had no aim but to get as far away as possible. I drank at a small stream and there I had the good fortune to fall in with an old hunter of English rather than Dutch extraction. He was a taciturn fellow, but he bound up my wounds and stayed with me until I was strong enough to walk. Then he gave me a few days supply of dried meat and left me.

"I had no impulse to rejoin my regiment, I simply wanted to have done with war and fighting. Day by day I made my way to the coast at Durban. The journey took over a year, and I had to beg my bread. Despite this I lived well enough: when people saw my raw and livid wounds they were racked with feelings of disgust and pity and gave me what I needed. In the first week of my travels a farmer's wife gave me some cast-off clothes so I no longer had to wear the tatters of my uniform.

"I worked my passage to Liverpool and made my way back to my home town. I could not bring myself to contact my parents – my mother had always been so proud of my handsome looks and my father, who has a very strong sense of duty, would despise a man who had run away from the enemy and then deserted his regiment. I preferred that they believed that I died fighting for my country.

"Instead, I contacted my darling Jenny. I had first approached her after a performance at the Prince of Wales theatre, where she played Helena in *A Midsummer Night's Dream*. We came to love one another, but I could not tell my parents of this as they would not consider an actress suitable for their only son. We had resolved to wait until after my military service when my position would be more secure, before we declared our love.

"When I arrived at her door, she took me in, maimed as I was, and shortly afterwards we married. I cannot find employment: people turn away at the sight of my face and wish to be rid of me. It is of no concern to them that I received my injuries in the Queen's service. I cannot even draw a soldier's pension as I deserted the colours. We were forced to depend on Jenny's earnings on the stage, and then she realised that she was to become a mother and we faced starvation, not only for ourselves but for our child.

"It was then that we struck on the idea of approaching my mother with a tale of communicating with my spirit. We knew that it was wrong, but after all it was my own family from which I was taking money. The scheme worked as well as we could have hoped and we have accumulated a little nest-egg. In time, we aimed at getting enough money to emigrate to one of the colonies – South Africa or Australia, perhaps. There I could become a farmer. My strength is unimpaired and my appearance would not matter in a country where a man's worth is not measured by his looks."

He ended his story. Holmes looked sympathetic, as indeed who would not after such a tale?

"There is no need to continue with this deception, which is painful for all concerned," he said firmly. "Having met your parents and most especially your father, I am convinced they would forgive you and welcome your wife. Your father loves you better than you know, Tom. Come, let Watson and I go with you to break the news as gently as may be."

The young couple looked at each other and wordlessly indicated their agreement. We left the house and found a four-wheeler to take us to the Murchison home. We simply told the servant that we wished to see Mr. and Mrs. Murchison on urgent business. When we came into their presence, they looked in shock and disbelief at the ravaged face of their son. Then Mrs. Murchison staggered forward. "Tom!" she cried, heartrendingly. "Tom!" She pressed him fiercely to her bosom.

Mr. Murchison stepped forward and grasped Thomas's hand. "Tom, my boy!" he said brokenly, "how is this possible?"

"Mother; father," said Thomas at last when their first joy was over, "can you ever forgive me? I have allowed you to believe I was dead; I have deserted the colours and I have taken money from you by a shameful trick."

"Of course we forgive you!" said Mrs. Murchison. "Just to have you back with us is worth everything we have." Mr. Murchison murmured his agreement.

"And now," continued Thomas, "may I further beg you to welcome into our family Jenny, who has become my wife and is bearing my child."

The elder Mrs. Murchison smiled tearfully. "A grandchild is all that is needed to crown our happiness," she said.

"Mr. Murchison," said Holmes, "you will not want the presence of Watson and myself at such a time. If you are satisfied with the outcome of the case we beg leave to withdraw."

Mr. Murchison immediately became the man of business. "I am not merely satisfied, but acknowledge the outcome has been happier than my wildest dreams," he said. "May I ask you to step into my study?"

We followed him to that room, where he produced his check-book and proceeded to write rapidly. "There Mr.

Holmes," he said, "I hope you will consider this adequate compensation for your labours."

Holmes glanced at the check and bowed. "You are most generous, sir," he said tucking it into his breast pocket.

"Not at all! It is I that am rewarded," said Murchison. He escorted us to the door personally, and wrung our hands as he said goodbye.

"But Holmes," I protested as we walked away, "why were you so certain that it was Thomas Murchison himself perpetrating this fraud, when we had no reason to suspect he was alive?"

"Always remember Watson that although it was very unlikely, it was not impossible that Thomas might have deserted his regiment or, shall we say, been captured and imprisoned by the enemy. I discounted those possibilities because Thomas' true voice was not used at the séances, and there seemed no reason for that to be so.

"But then you made your invaluable discovery of a local man who was at Majuba Hill. In itself this was quite unexpected – there were few enough survivors of that battle – but for one of them coincidentally to be a close friend of Thomas' and further now to be resident in Birmingham is stretching belief. The vital clue was your mentioning that the man had been injured in the jaw: this provided a clear explanation of the change in voice. Taken with the fact that Madame Beverley would have found herself pregnant at about the same time she contacted the elder Mrs. Murchison and the fact that she took money from no other source made the matter clear.

"The real honours of this case belong to you Watson, which is why it pains me to tell you that you will not be able to add this tale to your *oeuvre* as the officials at the War Department, being non-combatants themselves, are unsympathetic to those that flee from rifle-fire."

THE ADVENTURE OF THE CRICKETERS

EW of the cases in which Sherlock Holmes has been involved have been exposed to such a blaze of limelight as was given to the matter concerning two of the Gentlemen of England. One, Caspar Buchanan, had a wife who had been foully murdered; the other, Charles Thornton, was accused of the crime.

The adventure started early on a spring afternoon. Although it was almost time for lunch Holmes was still in his dressing gown and was sorting through the morning post; for my own part I was reading the paper. It was chilly enough at that season for Mrs. Hudson to have lit the fire in our sitting room. A knock came at our door and on being invited to enter, our landlady announced: "A young lady to see you Mr. Holmes. She says it's urgent."

"Pray show her in, Mrs. Hudson."

We rose to greet the lady, who was elegantly dressed although not, to my admittedly inexpert eye, at the very height of fashion. If she was surprised to see my friend in *deshabillé* she gave no sign of it.

"Good afternoon, gentlemen," she said, with a marked colonial accent. "My name is Mary Trevelyan and I've come to see you regarding a close friend who is in serious trouble with the police."

"Pray sit down, madam, and give me all the facts of the matter."

"Thank you. My friend is Mr. Caspar Buchanan, whose name is no doubt familiar to you."

"It is if you refer to the noted cricketer who so often opens the batting for the Gentlemen of England," said Sherlock Holmes.

"Exactly, Mr. Holmes. I first met him in Johannesburg last December when my father and I attended a match at the Wanderers ground between the Gentlemen and Transvaal.

Unlike many women I have a deep love for the game. The Gentlemen won the toss and elected to bat first. Caspar played a magnificently elegant game, making 103 before he was bowled. The match lasted four days, ending in an easy win for the visitors. On the last evening the committee gave a formal dinner for both teams. My father, George Trevelyan, sits on the committee so I attended the dinner and to my delight was seated next to Caspar. I have to confess that I was charmed by his elegant speech and manners.

"Johannesburg is a mining town and full of the most ruffianly characters. There are miners from all over the world; impoverished Afrikaners; natives that perform the labouring work; tradesmen that cater to the most depraved needs; gangsters that prey on them and all the dregs of civilization that have flocked there lured by the lust for gold. A civilized man is rare indeed. I spoke to Caspar all evening, almost completely ignoring, I regret to say, the gentleman on my right.

"We parted on the most amicable terms and next day he visited my father and myself – I should say that my dear mother died some years ago – and took tea with us. To my chagrin it became clear during the conversation that Caspar was married, and I need not say that there are no circumstances in which I would compromise myself by associating with a married man.

"Next day we received a note of thanks from him for our hospitality and inviting us to visit him when we were next in London. My father travels annually to England to discuss business with his agents and even though I knew my partiality was hopeless, I could not bear the thought of never seeing Caspar again and asked my father if I could accompany him on his next visit."

"Pardon me," interrupted Holmes, "but you have not yet informed me of your father's line of business."

"Of course: how remiss of me. He is in fact a mine-owner. We have a sizeable concession a few miles to the west of Johannesburg."

"Gold?"

"Yes. As I was saying, I asked my father if I could go to London with him and he was delighted to agree. I have in fact visited before with both my parents, but I was little more than a child at the time and I convinced myself that apart from any other matter I should renew my acquaintance with the greatest city on earth.

"A few months later, the arrangements were made and we took the *Arundel Castle* from Cape Town to Southampton, landing only yesterday morning. A few hours later we were in London and are currently staying at Brown's Hotel in Mayfair."

"Is that where your father usually stays when in town?"

"No. Caspar made the arrangements. Brown's is close to his apartments in South Audley Street."

"I see. Please go on."

"Caspar very kindly met us at the docks in Southampton and escorted us by train to Waterloo and then on to Brown's. While we were taking tea to refresh ourselves after the journey, we made some arrangements for the following days. My father asked him if he would join him that evening at the Savile Club, a short distance away, where he is a guest member. Caspar declined, pleading a previous engagement, but as I was seeing him out, he begged me in a whisper to meet him for dinner. I was weak enough to agree and he called for me that evening, after my father had gone to his club. Caspar had arranged a private room at a restaurant nearby and we talked all evening about our predicament. He protested that he loved me in a way that he had never loved his wife, but I am not dead to propriety and told him that he had taken vows before God and man and I would never be the cause of his breaking them. Finally, he announced that with deep grief he would accept my decision. As it was getting late, there was a danger that my father would return before I did, so he accompanied me back to Brown's, taking an emotional farewell at the door."

"Early this morning, the hotel manager knocked at my door and informed me that the police wanted to speak to me. I was bewildered, but roused my father and met the officer in a room the hotel provided."

"Who was the officer?" asked my friend.

"Inspector Gregory of Scotland Yard."

"Ah, yes. I am familiar with that gentleman. An extremely competent man, if perhaps a little lacking in imagination."

"The inspector gave us the dreadful news that Caspar's wife, Agnes, had been murdered last night. Caspar had been under suspicion, but had told the police that he was dining with me at the time. I was forced to admit that I had been alone with him until late at night. My father was furious that I had deceived him in this way and that I had dined unaccompanied with a married man. Inspector Gregory questioned me closely and took notes and finally said that he would probably want to talk to me again. I fear he is not fully satisfied. I have come to beg you to look into the matter Mr. Holmes and convince the police that Caspar could not possibly have been the murderer."

"The time you parted with him may be important. What can you say of that?"

"The mantel clock at the restaurant said eleven o'clock. Caspar pulled out his own watch and declared it to be correct. We then took a few minutes donning our cloaks and walking back to the hotel."

"Thank you Miss Trevelyan," said Holmes. I think I have what I need for the present. I will talk to the other people involved and contact you at Brown's."

The lady thanked us prettily and was shown out. At the door we found a young man waiting for us impatiently. He visibly restrained himself until we had completed our farewells but then accosted Holmes at once.

"Mr. Sherlock Holmes? My name is Vincent Greenford. I must speak with you on a matter of the greatest urgency."

"Of course. Please come into my room. This, by the way, is my companion Dr. Watson before whom you may speak freely."

We entered the sitting room and took our seats again.

"Now, can I take it you have come to consult me regarding the murder of Mrs. Agnes Buchanan?"

The young man started violently. "How on earth did you guess?" he exclaimed.

Holmes gestured towards his tie which was in the colours of purple, black and gold. "You wear the tie of the Incogniti cricket club. We are all aware that several members of that famous club also play for the Gentlemen of England and this coupled with the murder last night of Mrs. Buchanan led me to make the connection."

The young man shook his head in amazement. "You are quite right, sir. In fact, I'm the team captain and as I'm sure you also know, one of our players, Charles Thornton, is accused of the crime."

I regret to say that my friend's vanity would not allow him to admit his previous ignorance of this fact, and he simply nodded in reply.

"Of course, you don't know Charles as we do, but I can say for an absolute certainty that old Buns would never do anything of the kind."

"Buns?"

"That's his nickname from when we were at Eton together. He was fielding at long leg, near the road. The baker's boy happened to be passing and he bought a bun and started munching at it. Just then, a high ball was hit to him and he crammed the bun into his mouth before diving for the catch."

"I see. And why should the police suspect him particularly?"

The young man looked uneasy. "Well," he said finally, "it is a bit of an open secret that he was soft on Mrs. Buchanan, even though she's a fair bit older. Whenever he saw her at matches or our get-togethers he was always most attentive and she was all smiles for him. I can't say that Caspar liked it much. Also, Buns does have a bit of a temper, don't-you-know. Last season there was a carter he beat senseless for hitting his nag when it couldn't shift the load. And he's not shy of a knockabout with anyone that argues with him."

Holmes lifted his eyebrows. "I see," he murmured. "I think I will take your case, Mr. Greenford. It links in nicely with another matter I have in hand. If you could write down your address I expect to be in touch in a few days."

"That's splendid," said the young sportsman. "If you could just prove to the police that Buns couldn't possibly be guilty, that's all we need. It was probably a passing burglar or something, so it shouldn't be difficult. Can I ask you to work quickly, Mr. Holmes? He's the best fast bowler we've got and we really need him for the opening fixture against Sussex in a week's time. Also of course it will save money if you can finish the whole thing in a couple of days: I've arranged a levy from all the chaps to pay your fee, but none of us is what you might call flush."

"You can be sure that I will do my best," said Sherlock Holmes.

"Excellent! I'll expect to hear from you soon."

As we showed Mr. Greenford to the door, an older man came bustling up the stairs. We were certainly being kept busy that morning!

"I'm looking for Mr. Holmes," he said. To my surprise he had the same colonial accent as Miss Trevelyan.

"I am he," said Sherlock Holmes. "Pray come into my consulting room."

Our latest visitor was a strongly-built and sunburnt man. He was expensively dressed, but he seemed to wear his finery as if he were not used to it. We sat down and the client introduced himself. "My name is George Trevelyan," he said, "and I need your help for my daughter Mary, who's got herself into a bit of a fix. I'm not from hereabouts, but I've been recommended to you as someone who can find out things that others can't."

"I would hardly say that," replied my friend, "but I am aware that you are a mine-owner and that you arrived by the *Arundel Castle* from Cape Town yesterday morning and are currently staying at Brown's Hotel."

"Good heavens, Mr. Holmes!" exclaimed our visitor, "I've heard that your powers of reasoning are amazing, but this beats everything! To think that you can deduce all that simply from looking at me!"

"It is on occasion less difficult than it may appear," murmured Holmes.

"Well, you're properly modest Mr. Holmes, but you can't stop me being impressed. You're exactly the man I need. The thing is, my little Mary has got herself entangled with a married man. I never particularly liked the look of him myself, but Mary was dead set on him – we don't get many gentlemen in Johannesburg and his classy manners swept her off her feet. His name is Caspar Buchanan: he's one of the Gentlemen of England so you'll have heard of him. Mary had dinner with him last night and sometime that evening his wife was strangled. He's using my daughter as an alibi, but I don't believe he's innocent. Mary would never lie, so he must have had an accomplice. What I need you to do Mr. Holmes is to prove that Buchanan arranged to have his wife killed and send him to meet the hangman as he deserves."

"If he is indeed guilty, then the action you outline would be both a duty and a pleasure," said my friend. "But I will not conceal from you that I have heard of the murder and the police have arrested another man that they believe committed the crime on his own behest."

Mr. Trevelyan looked glum. "Well, I don't want you to pin the blame on an innocent man, but I've got to say I don't trust him. I think he's after my Mary and her money. I'm a widower and she's my only child. She'll be a very rich woman when I die: my mine has been producing 2,000 ounces a month since I introduced the cyanide process."

"I will begin work this very afternoon and I hope to have news for you soon. I will send a messenger to Brown's Hotel as soon as may be."

"My sincere thanks, Mr. Holmes. I know that if anyone can sort this out, it's you."

We ushered out our latest visitor, and I saw with relief that there was no-one else waiting for a consultation. After the door to our rooms was closed and we were alone, I coughed tactfully. "You appear to have accepted three clients with conflicting requirements, Holmes," I said. "I fear it will not be possible to please them all."

Sherlock Holmes gave an amused shrug. "You are no doubt right, Watson, but after all my ultimate duty is not to any client, but to the truth. Now I think we will interview Inspector Gregory who will have all the details of the crime: but first I must don something more formal than a dressing gown."

We took a hansom to Scotland Yard and asked to see the inspector. In short order we were conducted to his office and shook hands.

"It's a pleasure to see you again Mr. Holmes, and of course you too, Doctor. Please be seated."

"We have come to get further information regarding the murder of Mrs. Agnes Buchanan," said my friend, "and we understand you have charge of the case."

"Quite right, Mr. Holmes. Let me give you what we know to date." He took out his notebook and began to leaf through it. "The murder was first reported to us at twenty minutes past eleven last night. A constable who was on his beat in Grosvenor Square was approached by Mr. Caspar Buchanan and asked to accompany him to his apartments in South Audley Street. There he found the body of Mrs. Agnes Buchanan who appeared to have been strangled with a silk scarf that was still on her neck. In attendance was Dr. George Graveley who lives in the same collection of flats and had been summoned earlier by Mr. Buchanan. The doctor informed our constable that the woman was dead. The constable then asked Dr. Graveley and Mr. Buchanan to accompany him to Vine Street station where the matter was reported."

He broke off his reading to say, "I don't have to tell you that nine times out of ten when a woman is murdered it's the husband that did it. We took purely formal evidence from Dr. Graveley, but Mr. Buchanan was questioned until two o'clock the next morning. But then we got our own doctor's report." He had recourse again to his notebook. "The victim was examined at the site of the crime at ten minutes past midnight. The doctor described her as a woman of medium build, apparently in her mid-thirties. A silk scarf – probably her own - was wound tightly about her neck. The face was blackened and the tongue protruding. Rigor mortis was evident in her face, but not elsewhere. He partially removed her clothing and found discernible lividity on her back. The edge of a rug that had been underneath her had caused a wide whiter band to be seen across discoloured skin. The temperature was normal for this time of year and the doctor estimated that death had occurred at about ten o'clock that evening."

The inspector broke off again to discuss the findings. "You both have had a great deal of experience of this, so you know that rigor mortis usually starts about two hours after death, with the face, neck and shoulders first to show the effects. The lividity, caused by the blood pooling at the lowest point after the heart stops beating, starts to show itself within half an hour. Now by then Caspar Buchanan had given us his alibi that he was dining with a young woman until eleven o'clock. He's a well-known man so we thought it best to tell him he could go and stay at a hotel until we'd spoken to the young lady and searched the flat. Well, the most interesting thing that we found in the search was this." He picked up a piece of paper from his desk and passed it to us. It was a single line written across a sheet of plain notepaper and said: 'I must see you. I will come tonight – Charles'.

"Interesting," said my friend. "Where was this found?"

"Tucked behind the clock. Not hidden exactly, but unless you knew where to look you wouldn't guess it was there."

"And you deduced that the name referred to Charles Thornton?"

"We spoke to a few of Mrs. Buchanan's friends and two of them said that she had mentioned Mr. Thornton as being very attentive. We went round to his home and got samples of his handwriting: they match very well. So we arrested him and he's being questioned right now."

"Does he admit the note?"

"No. He says it's a forgery."

"Does he have an alibi?"

"Of a sort. He says he was at a boxing match near East Grinstead all evening, getting back about midnight. He went alone, so the only witnesses might be any of the spectators that happened to recognise him. Of course, prize-fighting is illegal so none of them are likely to come forward and even if they did I wouldn't trust the sort of ruffians you get at those shows."

Holmes pursed his lips. "I would say that your case is not as strong as one would like it to be."

Inspector Gregory nodded. "You're quite right, Mr. Holmes. We don't have any knock-down proof he was there. He denies he wrote the letter. The letter isn't dated, so in court his barrister will argue that it could have been there some time; although that's all my eye: a wife would never leave something like that where her husband might come across it. On the other hand, we don't have a clear motive for a murder. Thornton might yell at her; but murder her? That's not likely.

"But I can't get a good grip on Caspar Buchanan either. The motive's no problem and he and the girl used a private room with its own entrance separate from the regular diners, so no-one saw them come and go. Convenient, wouldn't you say? The girl's soft on him, so perhaps he persuaded her to lie, but I don't think so: she's not the sort of girl to cover up a murder."

"It has been suggested that the husband had an accomplice," said Holmes.

The Inspector shrugged. "Perhaps; although I've never heard of a man employing an assassin in this country. This isn't Corsica, where they say you can hire a killer and have change from a tenner."

My friend indicated his agreement. "Thank you for a very clear outline of the case, Inspector. Perhaps as he is on the premises we might be allowed to speak to Charles Thornton?"

"By all means, Mr. Holmes. I would be very interested in any conclusions you draw from his story."

We were led along a succession of dingy corridors to a small room in which a young man sat sullenly at a deal table opposite a uniformed constable.

"Afternoon, Albert," said Inspector Gregory. "Mr. Holmes here would like a word with our prisoner."

"As you say, sir," said Albert getting to his feet. Both officers left us alone with the man.

"Good afternoon, Mr. Thornton," said Holmes. "My name is Sherlock Holmes and this is my companion Dr. Watson. Mr. Vincent Greenford has asked us to do what we can for you."

"Damned decent of him. Vincent was always someone a chap could rely on."

"Indeed. Now I must have all the facts and so I must ask you to be as frank as possible with me regarding your relationship with Mrs. Buchanan."

"I give you my solemn word that there was absolutely nothing improper. I simply admired her greatly as a pure and matchless woman."

"You were never alone with her, or proposed that you be alone?"

"Good God, no! That letter is a damnable forgery."

"And yet it exists. Have you any idea why?"

Charles Thornton shook his head in bafflement. I was gaining the impression that whatever his skills on the cricket pitch he was not a man of great intellectual power.

"What is your opinion of Caspar Buchanan?"

"The man is an absolute bounder," said Thornton angrily. "He is completely unworthy of a woman such as her."

"These could be the slanders of an envious man," said Sherlock Holmes, provokingly.

Our young friend looked furious. "I can prove he's a liar," he said. "It's well known that he gives out that he went to Harrow when in fact it was some beastly private school in the Midlands. When he left there he got a captaincy in a local regiment no-one's ever heard of. He lasted about two years before he was asked to resign his commission because he was signing other officers' names in the mess book. They covered it up, but it's an open secret. If he hadn't caught Agnes' eye he'd be in trade by now. It's her money that lets him live like a gentleman."

"And yet I have heard no-one describe their marriage as unhappy."

Charles Thornton shrugged. "She kept him on a short leash and he knew what would happen if he made trouble. I suppose they had settled down together."

"I see. Now turning to your own movements yesterday, Inspector Gregory tells me you went to a prize-fight?"

"Quite correct. I always go to see any match I hear of. They're not held often these days – the police call it riotous assembly – but I tell you gentlemen, once you've seen the real thing; two men fighting it out with bare knuckles and the blood flowing, you'll never want to see a bout with the mittens again. A tout gave me a handbill in the street a few days ago about a match between Jem Mace and Ned O'Baldwin at The Bull in Forest Row. I took the train to East Grinstead, and walked a couple of miles to The Bull. There was a whole crowd of us got off the train, all laughing and joking as we went along. The Bull is well known as a fighting-house and the landlord is an old pugilist himself.

110

He'd roped off a ring in the field behind his house. The fight was due to start at three and before then we all gathered in the public house to drink and talk. I fell into a conversation with a few others of the fancy and got the latest news. Jem Mace is five foot eleven and eleven-six and Ned O'Baldwin is a giant at six foot five and all of thirteen stone, but Jem is fast on his feet and more scientific. The betting was fierce on both sides, I can tell you.

"At three or thereabouts we all trooped out to the field. The two pugilists came in to great cheers. They squared up to each other and danced about for a while, each getting the measure of the other. They both lashed out a couple of times but with no effect. Then suddenly Jem dived in and got two good ones on O'Baldwin's ribs. You could see the red marks of his knuckles on the skin. O'Baldwin got angry and rushed in with great hammer-blows that knocked Mace to the ground. As he struggled to his feet, O'Baldwin wrapped an arm around his neck and started punching his face with great, short blows. That's the glory of the London Rules; you can seize your opponent by any part except the breeches or below the waist. The Queensbury Rules have taken all the manliness out of the sport.

"Well, Jem wrenched himself out of the hold, but he was hurt: you could hardly see his face, the claret ran so free. O'Baldwin came in for the kill, but Jem grabbed his arm as he swung the punch and tripped him. Ned's a big man and it wasn't easy for him to get to his feet. Every time he struggled up on one knee Jem hit him on the side of the face. He got a couple of good hits on his left eye and kept punching at it. O'Baldwin was roaring like a bull but could do nothing about it. Finally he got up and they started trading punches again, but you could see it was as good as over. Jem kept dancing around to his blind side and landing blows on the head. O'Baldwin got slower and slower and Mace kept up the attack. At the last, Ned dropped to his knees and stayed there. After thirty seconds, the referee declared Jem the winner. How we cheered! We carried him

111

shoulder high into the public house and plied him with drinks. The bets were settled – I won a few pounds – and we drank and talked until late. At about ten o'clock I realized I had better get back to London if I was to catch the last train and walked to the station. The next morning I slept late until I was awoken by the police. The rest you know."

"O'BALDWIN GOT ANGRY AND RUSHED IN
WITH GREAT HAMMER-BLOWS."

"Who backed the fight?"

"Felix Larkin is Ned's backer, but I never knew who backed Jem; he didn't seem to be present."

"Isn't that rather unusual?"

The young man pondered this. "I suppose you're right. I've never heard of a backer that wasn't there cheering on his man. Especially with a purse of a thousand pounds at stake."

"Perhaps he had his own reasons for remaining anonymous," suggested my friend. "It may not be of any importance, but it is strange all the same. I think I have all I need for the present, Mr. Thornton. I will work as quickly as may be to prove your innocence."

Charles Thornton thanked us warmly and we took our leave of him.

As we walked down the road, the hawkers were crying the early edition of the *Evening Standard.* "'Orrible murder of cricketer's wife!" shouted one urchin. "Fixtures may be cancelled!" He seemed to be doing brisk business with both lovers of gore and of cricket.

We walked the short distance to Charing Cross Hospital where we were admitted to the mortuary. Under a sheet lay the body of Mrs. Agnes Buchanan. The attendant removed the covering and we saw the agony of her death. The face was empurpled and the mouth gaping open. The body had been left exactly as it had been found to await the post-mortem. Around the neck was a scarf drawn so tightly into the flesh that it was only just possible to see that its colour was blue. Behind the head protruded the incongruous sight of a common fireside poker which had been used to twist the ligature tight. My friend turned the body gently to one side then the other to view the details. After a short time he said, "There is little to be learned here that we have not already been apprised of. Let us take our leave."

After expressing our thanks to the attendant, we walked away in silence, both subdued by the evidence of mortality we had witnessed. Finally, Sherlock Holmes roused himself. "There is one final party to all this, Watson, and that is Caspar Buchanan himself. Let us delay our tea for a while and visit him. I would assume that by now he will be back at his home in South Audley Street."

We took a cab to Mayfair and sent up our names. In a short time Mr. Buchanan appeared in the entrance hall and greeted us cordially. "Please come up to my rooms, gentlemen," he said. "Alas, I cannot offer you any sort of hospitality in the circumstances, but I shall be glad to answer your questions."

His flat was on the second floor. We all seated ourselves and Caspar Buchanan offered around cigarettes. We both refused, but he took one himself and puffed at it during our conversation. "Now, gentlemen, how may I help you?"

"I have already had many of the facts from Inspector Gregory who has taken charge of the case," said Sherlock Holmes. "I am principally interested in what you can tell me of your fellow team-member Charles Thornton."

"A hot-headed young fool," replied Mr. Buchanan decisively. "I can of course understand a young man's admiration of a woman with the qualities of my late wife, but his attentions went beyond politeness to the point of insolence. He is well known to be impulsive and to have a fondness for violent sports such as prize-fighting. I would not put anything beyond him when his temper is roused."

"You will have been told that a note from him to your wife was found on these very premises."

Caspar Buchanan shook his head in perplexity. "Agnes was a very generous and good-hearted woman. It is possible that she agreed to see him in private for a time to make matters clear to him. I will never believe that she had anything more than a concern for his youth. It may well be that her rejection of his advances drove him to fury. I do not know: I leave the matter to the police."

Holmes and Caspar Buchanan discussed the matter for some little time, then Holmes rose to his feet. "I cannot thank you enough for allowing me to question you at this difficult period," he said. "May I give you my card and ask you to contact me if you should remember anything further that might help my investigations."

"I will indeed." He took the card, glanced at it briefly and put it in his breast pocket. He then courteously accompanied us to the street door.

114

As we walked away, my friend made an observation. "You will have noted, Watson, that Buchanan is left-handed. He smokes his cigarettes with that hand and when I offered my card he took it with his left hand."

"Certainly," I said. "He is well-known as a left-handed batsman."

"Ah, I was not aware of that. The world of amateur sport is so clean and pure that my duties seldom impinge upon it. The ruffians that abound at the turf and the ring take much more of my time." He pondered for a space then continued. "I believe it is likely that Agnes Buchanan was strangled by a left-handed person. The scarf about her neck is twisted in an anti-clockwise direction. That direction comes much more naturally to a left-hander."

"So the assassin was also left-handed?" I said baffled. "Is that not a great coincidence?"

"In terms of pure chance about one in ten." He said little more until we were back in our rooms, when he proposed: "Let me ring for Mrs. Hudson to bring us some tea, and then I will smoke a pipe or two and consider the problem from all its aspects." In due course the tea arrived and was consumed. My friend walked over to his pipe-rack to make his selection. I saw him hesitate between his old, oily clay pipe and his battered and scorched briar. The long cherry-wood pipe with its cooler smoke he tended to reserve for our discursive conversations in the evenings and I never saw him use the curiously-carved meerschaum, which I believe was a souvenir of an old case. Finally he settled on the clay; stuffed it with the strong and coarse tobacco he favoured; leaned back in his chair and began to puff meditatively. For my part I simply sat quietly, not even daring to read in case the rustle of the pages should disturb him. I believe I fell into a half-doze before I was wakened by him walking over to the bookshelf and selecting some work of reference. Flicking through the pages he read for a few seconds, then closed the book with a decisive thump and replaced it.

"Well, Watson, I believe I have a possible answer, and if you are willing to stretch your legs with a stroll in Hyde Park we can test my reasoning."

"Of course!" I said heartily.

We walked south to Oxford Street, and a short distance along that road to Speakers' Corner. There we entered Hyde Park and delighted in the fresh green leaves which were appearing at that time. My friend chose to walk parallel to the border with Park Lane and we strolled along at a gentle pace. I noted that he was looking at the foot of the trees, almost all of which in that area were young specimens with boles no more than a foot in diameter. After ten minutes or so we began to approach Rotten Row, the sandy ride that follows the southern end of the park. There were a few horsemen on the track, giving their steeds some evening air and a respite from the hard roads of London. At the edge of the ride and close to where we walked was a stand of huge plane trees. Sherlock Holmes approached them and inspected the base of each tree in turn. Finally he gave an exclamation of satisfaction and gestured at the earth. I looked and saw a few cigarette stumps, all of similar appearance, presumably dropped by an idler who had spent some time there; perhaps talking or waiting for a companion. I looked questioningly at my friend.

"I have mentioned before my little monograph upon the characteristic ash produced by a hundred and forty forms of cigar, cigarette and pipe tobacco," he said. "Here however, the problem is much simpler as we have the tobacco itself." He picked up one of the stumps and crumbled it gently in his fingers then raised it to his nose. "Latakia," he pronounced. "A very distinctive tobacco from the eastern Mediterranean which is cured with aromatic woods. The same tobacco in fact that Mr. Buchanan was smoking when we visited him.

"The stumps are not noticeably damp, and we have had a little rain in the last twenty-four hours, but on the other hand we are in the shelter of the tree. I would estimate from

116

the freshness of the tobacco that at some time yesterday he came here and smoked cigarettes for up to an hour."

I groped for understanding. "He came here to smoke and think matters over before he joined Mary Trelawney for dinner?" I hazarded. "But why here?"

"I believe there is another explanation, but we will return to our rooms and send a message to Miss Trelawney to join us. I fancy a little more information from her will give us the answer."

An hour later we rose to our feet as Mary Trelawney was announced. "Good afternoon, madam," said my friend. "Please be seated. I have asked you to join us as I have two further questions which I believe will clear the matter up. Can I first ask you if immediately after you and Caspar Buchanan had left the restaurant he had to return for any reason?"

Miss Trelawney gasped in shock. "However did you know that, Mr. Holmes? Yes, you are quite right: as we walked down the steps from our room he announced that he had forgotten his gloves and would have to go back for them. He was no more than a few seconds."

"As I expected. The second question is that having returned to your room at Brown's Hotel, did you immediately retire for the night?"

"Yes, I did. It must have been well past half-past eleven, which is about the time that I normally go to bed and I felt tired after such an eventful day."

"Again as I expected. Thank you madam: I think you have given me the solution. I find from Whitaker's Almanac that a few years ago the Transvaal, the Orange Free State and the Cape Colony agreed on a uniform time that is one and a half hours ahead of Greenwich Mean Time. You had landed from the steamship that morning, where ship's time corresponded to the port of departure, and you believe that you retired at what in South Africa was one o'clock in the morning. You should therefore have felt extremely sleepy rather than as you describe it, normally tired.

"What I believe happened is that Caspar Buchanan visited the restaurant shortly before he met you, ostensibly no doubt to check that the arrangements were satisfactory, but in reality to put the mantel clock at least an hour forward. At the end of the meal he announced to you it was eleven o'clock when in fact it was perhaps only ten. It was necessary for him to turn back on the stairs to re-set the mantel clock as otherwise the staff would discover the discrepancy. I have observed that, like many ladies of leisure, you do not carry a watch, and no doubt Mr. Buchanan had made the same observation."

As my friend developed his argument an expression of horror grew on Mary Trelawney's face. She clenched her fists so tight that the knuckles whitened.

Without pity, Sherlock Holmes continued. "He went home and ruthlessly strangled his wife. Knowing that suspicion would inevitably fall upon him, he had arranged to confuse the issue by implicating another man, a known admirer of his wife. This man was a keen follower of the prize-ring, so he organised a fight to take place on the day you were to arrive, providing the purse from his own pocket and hoping his mark would take the bait. He also forged a note purporting to be from that man and left it at the scene. I must tell you that some years ago he was obliged to resign his commission following allegations of forgery.

"He then had the problem that he must stay out of sight for a long period before he could 'discover' the body and raise the alarm. Where could he go? As one of the Gentlemen of England his face would be recognised by many. He could not walk the streets or go to a public house. What he did was walk across Park Lane and lurk in the trees that border Rotten Row. He calculated correctly that no-one seeing a man in evening dress apparently alone with his thoughts late at night would wish to disturb him. As he waited, he smoked a number of cigarettes. I discovered the stumps of cigarettes of the same tobacco that he commonly smokes at the foot of one of the larger trees."

Miss Trelawney's distress at all this was more than I could bear. I stepped forward to proffer my aid, but she waved me away brusquely.

Taking control of herself she stood firmly upright. "Your arguments are convincing, Mr. Holmes and no doubt you will pass on your conclusions to the appropriate authorities. As for me, I shall not stay to give evidence at a sordid trial and put a hempen rope around Caspar's neck. I shall engage a special to the coast immediately and then sail for South Africa.

"Meanwhile, as you have worked at my behest, I must pay what I owe." Reaching into her purse she pulled out almost at random a number of massy gold coins and flung them on the table. "I believe this will cover your fee Mr. Holmes. Good day to you both." With no further words she turned and left, our bows of farewell being perforce directed at her retreating back.

"Well, Watson, I fancy I have not done too badly," said Holmes philosophically, as he pocketed the coins. "Two of my three clients have what they asked for, and the third, no matter what her present distress, has escaped marrying a murderer. However, you will oblige me by not chronicling the matter: there are those that might doubt that my only motive was the love of the game."

THE ADVENTURE OF THE RUSSIAN ANARCHIST

HILE standing at the window of our lodgings one day, idly watching the bustle in Baker Street below me, I became aware of a light cabriolet being driven at a smart clip from the south. It crossed over the road and pulled up outside our door.

"Holmes!" I said with some excitement. "You are about to receive a message from the Foreign Office."

My friend looked up from his armchair where he was comfortably settled with his newspaper and laughed. "If you spy a visitor dressed up to resemble a glorified postman in a blue double-breasted frockcoat; Oxford Mixture trousers with a red stripe and a cap with the Royal cypher on the front you must not expect praise for your deductive abilities in declaring him a Foreign Office messenger! But let us see what he brings: I have no doubt it will be of interest!"

We waited in some impatience until Mrs. Hudson announced the man. He sprang to attention and gave us an officious salute. "I have a message for a Mr. Sherlock Holmes," he stated.

"I am he," said my companion taking the letter offered. He opened it and read the contents. "Hm!" he said, "Lord Hawkesbury asks me to attend him 'at my early convenience'. I think we can take it that means immediately. I hope you will be able to accompany me, Doctor?"

"With the greatest pleasure!"

We dismissed the messenger and took a cab to Whitehall. After giving in our names we were escorted with surprising promptness to the offices of the Secretary of State for Foreign Affairs.

"Good afternoon, gentlemen," he greeted us. "It is most kind of you to come so quickly. Please be seated."

Holmes and I sat as invited, but Lord Hawkesbury remained standing and seemed somewhat ill at ease. "I have invited you here Mr. Holmes on a most delicate matter," he said. "I am of course aware both of your noted abilities and of your discretion. Lord Holdhurst has informed me of the service you did our country in a matter concerning a naval treaty and I have every confidence that the matter I am about to discuss with you will remain entirely confidential."

My friend inclined his head at this.

The Minister continued. "The affair concerns the safety of representative of a most important European power. Matters between our countries are in a very delicate position. Fighting has broken out between two bordering African colonies of our respective empires, waged by troops from both our nations. Unless some agreement can be reached in a short time we may well find ourselves at war. This gentleman has been sent by his government to discuss ways to resolve our differences. As Secretary for Foreign Affairs I am charged with reaching a satisfactory settlement. You will understand therefore that it is of the highest importance that the envoy have no cause to complain of his reception in this country or feel in any way threatened."

"Certainly. And why should he?"

Lord Hawkesbury looked grim. "There are persons, gentlemen, to whom all government is unacceptable. They say that they fight to make men free of any authority, but of course if their efforts were ever crowned with success we should not have freedom but rather oppression by wicked men who would have no curbs on their actions. These persons will seize any chance to cause disruption and undermine the people's confidence in the established order. In this case they have a unique opportunity whereby one well-placed assassination could cause a major war.

"Scotland Yard has been fully briefed on the situation, and has assigned a team of men to investigate threats to the diplomat's safety. They are led by Inspector Lestrade, with whom I believe you are acquainted. Now I have, it goes without saying, every confidence in the competence of the regular police, but in these special circumstances –" He broke off here, apparently unsure as to how to continue.

Holmes made a negligent gesture. "Perhaps they would appreciate some support in a matter involving a foreign dignitary."

Lord Hawkesbury seized on this at once. "Certainly. Certainly. You have hit the matter exactly. Someone such as yourself with your broader experience of the continent may well bring valuable insights."

"You honour me with your confidence in my abilities sir, but I have to point out that I cannot be fully effective in such circumstances where there may be dozens of men who have the will and the means to carry out such an atrocity. In these cases the police with their ability to call on a large number of watchers is the best weapon you have."

"In general I would agree completely. But in this particular case we believe that because of the importance of the undertaking, those who oppose us have banded together and approached a foreign anarchist with wide experience of 'propaganda by deed' as they call it in their detestable jargon. In plain words, the shooting and bombing of innocent people. This agent is named Prince Peter Kropotkin. He is a Russian who until recently has resided in Paris. He is notorious in anarchist circles. Although nothing can be proved to the stringency required by a court of law, he is thought to be the guiding hand behind the recent violent demonstrations in Rheims and Montceau; the bomb attacks in Lyon and other outrages. Six days ago this man abruptly left Paris and is now in London."

"But are you quite certain that his visit is connected with the visit of your envoy?"

"Let us say that we have a very strong suspicion. As you know, the Parisian police have at their disposal a vast number of spies and *mouchards* that bring them detailed intelligence, and we are reliably informed that Prince Peter's departure followed the visit of a mysterious Russian person. He knew little French and spoke to the boarding-house keeper in good English. This person arrived after the diplomat's visit had been arranged and Prince Peter left for England soon after. The coincidences in dates are too strong to be discounted."

"May I ask if this diplomatic visit is generally known?" asked my friend.

Lord Hawkesbury's mouth tightened. "I understand your point Mr. Holmes. No, it was not generally known and therefore we must conclude that there is a person in my Department who is passing information to the anarchists. My tasks for you Mr. Holmes are both vital to our country: to frustrate any action taken against an honoured guest and to identify the informer in my service."

"Do you know of Prince Peter's current whereabouts?"

"Yes. He makes no secret at all of his movements. Indeed, this would be a fruitless task as he is watched so closely. He has a suite of rooms in the Savoy hotel. Inspector Lestrade's men have him under close observation and he cannot meet anyone without it being known. His room and luggage have been searched; his letters are opened and read at the post office and he is followed everywhere. He does nothing to thwart this activity and it seems in fact that their activities amuse him."

"Does he have visitors?

"Many. Also he dines almost every night in society. I regret to say that the fashionable decadence of our age finds an echo, however faint, in his activities."

"Why do you not simply arrest him on some charge or other? If you can keep him in the cells for a few weeks then release him, saying that there has been a regrettable misunderstanding, your problem is surely solved."

Lord Hawkesbury's lips pursed. "As Foreign Secretary I have few powers within the borders of this country. Instructions of such a nature would have to come from the Secretary of State for Home Affairs. Most unfortunately, he does not agree with my assessment of the situation. He points out quite correctly that the Russian nobility is closely allied with our own – indeed the Queen herself has the late Tsar as her godfather – and we would seriously offend them by arresting a member of the aristocracy. He claims that my fears are a chimera conjured up by the notoriously excitable French and precipitate action could well endanger our large and growing trade with Russia. And in conscience I cannot deny this last point. Indeed so greatly has trade grown that we have had to employ three extra clerk translators in my ministry."

I said nothing but one aspect of the matter became clear to me: the premier was in poor health and was expected to retire at the next election. Lord Hawkesbury and the Home Secretary were considered the leading candidates for his position. How infuriating that the safety of our country should be put into the balance by petty rivalry!

"It is clear that Prince Peter does not throw the bombs himself," mused my friend, "or he would by now have been brought to justice. His is the mind that plans and gives instructions to the fanatic that perpetrates the crime. Your instructions therefore imply that I must find the people he selects, organises, instructs and inspires."

Holmes sat back in his chair and placed the tips of his fingers together in the manner characteristic of him. "I cannot hide from you, sir, that the matter is of extreme difficulty. The anarchist has all the advantages. You cannot ask your diplomat to skulk about and nor would he compromise his dignity by doing so. He must go by the regular route and meet the regular people. The perpetrator has ample opportunity to spy out the lay of the land; make himself secure; choose his weapons at leisure and consider all avenues of escape."

Lord Hawkesbury almost so forgot himself as to wring his hands; instead he turned abruptly and looked out over St. James Park, doubtless considering the ruin of his career and reputation if Prince Peter or his myrmidons should succeed. He would inevitably be execrated as a man who had failed in his duty and thereby precipitated an avoidable war.

"You are of course right, Mr. Holmes, and I can only ask you to do your best. You have merely to ask for anything you should need. In addition, Inspector Lestrade will be instructed to give you every cooperation."

"I will naturally exert myself to the utmost. Is your diplomat in London at present?"

"No. Most fortunately like many of his countrymen he is fond of shooting, so we have taken him down to Inverness-shire for a week of the grouse season, professing that the discussion of our differences can better be conducted in a relaxing atmosphere. In such a remote region, a stranger would be noticed immediately. We therefore believe him to be safe for the moment. My Under-Secretary together with his assistant are going through the matters of detail and keeping me informed by wire. It is a complex matter and at the unhurried pace we are setting, we can reasonably hope to keep him in North Britain for ten days. After that, he must return to London and there will be some days of going back and forth between here and his embassy before the matter can be settled. If you have not succeeded in identifying the assassins by then, this will be the time of maximum danger."

"Well then, we have a little time in hand," said Sherlock Holmes. "Watson and I will investigate the matter and report back to you as soon as may be."

We took our leave of the minister and returned to Baker Street.

"Facts!" said my friend, "we must have facts before we can act. Let us begin by looking up our man in my index." Here he referred to the now voluminous mass of biographies; descriptions of events; notes on experiments and apparatus and other such miscellanea that he added to whenever something caught his eye and seemed worthy of note.

A little rummaging through a tottering pile on the sideboard produced a well-stuffed foolscap envelope. Holmes emptied its contents on to the table and began leafing through them.

"Prince Peter Kropotkin or more correctly, Pyotr Alexeyevich Kropotkin. He became a member of the Corps of Pages at the Russian court at the age of fifteen. As a young man he joined the army as an officer with the Siberian Cossacks. He was charged with leading a geographical survey and found the task congenial.

"On his discharge he travelled to the Jura Mountains in Switzerland, where he came in contact with anti-authoritarian thinkers and was converted to their espousal of anarchism and distribution of property according to need.

"A short time later he launched the journal *L'Avant-Garde* which called for 'propaganda by deed'. There is a cutting from that periodical here, Watson, which I might translate as: 'We are for the violent way. Let us go for the guns hanging on the walls of our attics.'

"As the Secretary for Foreign Affairs has already informed us, he is considered the guiding hand behind a number of assassinations and violent demonstrations. His military training has left him notably cool in a crisis; some might even say callous. There is an anecdote recorded here that he was once relaxing at a café as his bomb exploded in the next street. A waiter exclaimed that the noise had come from the Luxembourg Palace. Kropotkin took a sip of his absinthe and replied: 'I think you'll find it came from the *Café de l'Odéon*.' "

"The man is a monster!" I expostulated.

"I cannot disagree with you," replied Sherlock Holmes calmly. "But he does have the qualities of a high intelligence and great daring. Together with many years of experience he is a dangerous enemy. I fear Lestrade will hardly be a match for such a man, Nevertheless, let us pay the Inspector a visit and see what he has discovered."

We found Lestrade in his office which was bustling with activity. Uniformed constables and detectives in plain clothes were coming and going. Lestrade himself was in an ebullient mood. "It makes a very pleasant change to be given everything I've asked for and more," he confided. "We've been able to keep his Highness under constant observation both day and night. I doubt he's able to as much as scratch his nose without one of my men getting it down in writing."

"And have they noticed anything of more significance?" murmured my friend.

"Not a thing!" replied Lestrade cheerfully. "Between ourselves, gentlemen, I think Lord Hawkesbury has got a bee in his bonnet about his Highness. We've followed him for days and he does the ordinary round of a man of his position. He meets nobody that isn't – well, I won't say respectable, because he meets a lot of modern literary men whose morals are not what they should be if you ask me – but nobody you'd call dangerous; anarchists and such. It's obvious isn't it that a man high in society like himself isn't going to do anything to change the established order. He just likes a bit of raffish company, and after all, what's so wrong in that?

"On the other hand," he continued, holding up an admonitory finger, "it doesn't do to be complacent. It occurred to me that we're giving all our attention to foreigners when we've got plenty of troublemakers that were born right here. Now I've got the constables I've been able to what you might call interpret my instructions a little to keep an eye on them. It's not generally known, but there are groups of men that claim they're as patriotic as anything but still want to bring down the government. They're called Jacobites and they think the Royal family are usurpers and the Stuarts should still be on the throne – something to do with William of Orange being a foreigner. I've found that they're all over the place and they're well organised."

He produced his notebook and began to leaf through it. "So far I've been able to plant my men in the Order of the White Rose; the Legitimist Club; the Society of King Charles the Martyr; the White Cockade Club; the Society of the Red Carnation and the Order of Saint Germaine. Every man-jack of them wants to overthrow the constitution. That's where the danger lies, Mr. Holmes. They're mainly

128

gentlemen, so they've got the money and the brains. If they should start using dynamite they'll be a hundred times worse than any anarchist. But now that I've got my men listening at all their meetings I can guarantee that's not going to happen."

"I confess I had imagined the Jacobites were simply romantic eccentrics," conceded my friend.

Lestrade laughed complacently, "Well, you can't be expected to think of everything, Mr. Holmes. But in this case I think I can safely say the regular police have the matter well in hand."

Despite this clear hint, Holmes was insensitive enough to make careful arrangements for contacting the police at short notice. Lestrade undertook to leave exact directions as to his whereabouts whenever he should leave his office.

Back at Baker Street we discussed what action we should take. "The assassination of a prominent and well-guarded figure," explained Sherlock Holmes, "requires complex planning. An adept assassin will ensure that he has many times the number of men one might think he would need. You will recall that in the murder of the late Tsar three separate assassins were identified. They waited at a point where the procession had to slow for a bridge. The first bomb was ineffective and the attacker was overwhelmed by the guards, but the second threw the bomb which killed his Imperial Majesty. It was later found that yet a third assassin was waiting in the event that the first two failed.

"The matter at hand, which involves persons from three countries, cannot be arranged in a moment. Instructions cannot be muttered as an aside while brushing past an appearing bystander. Having summoned their master, the anarchists will want to meet numerous times to discuss and to argue. Conflict is in the nature of the anarchist: in the end each anarchist state would consist of one man. And yet the assiduous Lestrade would have told us at once of any meetings. So, where can they meet? How are instructions and questions passed back and forth?"

"The waiters perhaps?" I suggested.

"Possibly so. Many waiters are foreigners and the Savoy is a very modern hotel; none of its servants can be completely above suspicion. These matters must be arranged somehow, and we must find out how. Lestrade observes from outside, but we must break into the charmed circle."

"That will not be easy."

"Indeed: but one step at a time, Doctor. Firstly we must arrange a meeting with his Highness. I think it essential to get the measure of our man. From there we must gain his confidence and from there meet his acquaintances and from there we may be in a position to identify the plotters."

Holmes disappeared the next day but buttonholed me the following morning. "How would you like to be an anarchist, Watson?" he said, "One who is willing to risk his life and liberty for freedom."

"Would I need a disguise?" I asked doubtfully.

"Not at all! You will remain a doctor, but one who has been moved by the plight of the oppressed. There is no point in approaching our man without an introduction: he would immediately be suspicious, whatever the circumstances. But if we can provide ourselves with a background the matter becomes possible. I have made a few enquiries and I believe there is someone that can help us. Would you accompany me to Paddington?"

"Of course!" I replied heartily.

We strolled along the Marylebone Road for twenty minutes and at the end of that time Holmes led me through a maze of narrow streets near the railway line. At the end of journey we turned into a small and grimy yard. A saddler's premises occupied one side of it but seemed to be doing little business. Holmes indicated a flight of steps on one side of the building leading to an upper level.

"Up here I understand," he said.

He led the way up the steps and knocked on the door. To my surprise it was opened by a young lady of presentable dress and manner. She had rather severe features and a pair of oxford spectacles perched on a thin nose.

"What can I do for you, gentlemen?" she enquired formally.

Holmes bowed. "My name is Sherlock Holmes and this is my good friend Dr. John Watson. We have long been supporters of the cause in what one might call a theoretical way, but have recently come to feel that nothing will be achieved without practical help. We have therefore come to you to ask if there are any ways that we might assist in your undertaking."

"Please come in."

We entered the premises which I saw was a small printing-office. The room was piled with bundles of newspapers; boxes of type and various pieces of battered machinery. At its centre stood an ink-splattered hand press. On one side was a desk piled high with papers. Seated at it was a very pretty young person who looked up enquiringly at our entrance.

"I am Cassandra Stevens," said the girl who had received us, "and this is my sister Jane. Jane: these gentlemen have offered to help in our work."

Jane smiled in the sweetest possible manner. "We can always use willing hands," she said.

Holmes bowed again to Jane. "We are both literate men and would be well able to help with editing and proof-reading for example. We are also of adequate strength and would be more than happy to assist with tasks such as moving paper or lifting heavy items."

Cassandra appeared to soften somewhat at this. "We have found the physical exertion rather arduous," she conceded. "Will you join us for tea and we can discuss how you can best be of assistance?"

This was our introduction to the offices of the *Torch*, one of many small anarchist papers that flourished at that time. Cassandra and Jane were typical of the idealistic young people that made up much of the movement. They were the daughters of a man of letters and had received a liberal education. The sufferings of the poor in places such as Cuba and Russia had made a deep impression on them which they sought to draw attention to by 'propaganda by word'. I discovered later that there were many such magazines; some more radical than others. The *Torch* was of the gentler persuasion.

We spent most of the next few days at the *Torch*. One or both of us would be present assisting in any way we could. I sorted printers' pie; helped with deliveries; checked articles; ran errands and performed many other small jobs. In the course of this we came to know the others that frequented the offices; most of them merely loafers and hangers-on. There was a Polish count in shabby velvet who always wished to talk about his estates at Cracow that had been taken from him by the authorities. There was a number of 'working men' who seemed to have no work to do except disturb our tasks with rambling denunciations of the capitalist system. They included one loud drunkard who made work impossible with his ranting. Fortunately he could be enticed by small sums to return to the local public house. Jane's followers, usually effete would-be literary men, were also regular visitors. Holmes and I were the only ones apart from the girls who were actually prepared to do more than the occasional desultory task, and we rapidly gained their confidence.

When Holmes judged that the time was ripe, he casually raised the matter for which he had made these preparations. "Are you aware, ladies, that the noted revolutionary Prince Peter Kropotkin is visiting London at the moment?" he asked.

"Oh, indeed?" exclaimed Cassandra. "I have often heard tell of him. How wonderful it would be to meet and discuss the movement with someone so experienced!"

Holmes assumed a thoughtful expression. "It could be arranged, perhaps. I am informed by a friend that he regularly takes tea at the Café Royale. There is no reason why we should not also attend, and at least introduce ourselves."

It took very little to persuade the girls to make the visit. I believe their dedication to their work had left them missing the social scene and this was an excellent excuse to repair the lack. After lunch, they went home to change into their dinner gowns. While we waited, Holmes outlined his aims.

"Many men have been brought low by a pretty face, Watson, and I have hopes the trick will work again for us. Prince Peter is said to have an eye for the fair sex. We will see what he lets slip when flattered by our young ladies."

We all took a four-wheeler to Regent Street and entered the Café Royale; Holmes accompanying Cassandra and I Jane. I noticed Holmes speak quietly to the head waiter and slip something into his hand before we were escorted to a table that was well inside the restaurant, but some way from the musicians.

"This is where Prince Peter normally prefers to sit," explained my friend with a smile. "Far enough back so that he can observe comings and goings and quiet enough that he can talk to his friends. He is said to enjoy debate and to have a rapier wit."

We ordered tea and waited, the girls in some excitement. Perhaps twenty minutes later a waiter sidled up and murmured to Sherlock Holmes. "I understand you wished to be informed when Prince Peter arrived, sir. You can see his Highness now coming towards us."

Looking towards the door we saw a tall, thin man in impeccable evening dress. His face was narrow and of a very pale complexion with a rather prominent nose over a long waxed moustache. He held a fine silk top hat and a pair of gloves that I noted were dark red in colour. In all he seemed an elegant dandy.

"Now's your chance, Miss Jane," said Holmes with a smile.

"Oh no, I couldn't!" fluttered Jane.

"Don't be so silly, Jane," said her sister. "If you won't, I will!"

' "PRINCE PETER KROPOTKIN, I BELIEVE?" SHE SAID'

With that she boldly got to her feet and intercepted our quarry. "Prince Peter Kropotkin, I believe?" she said.

The Russian smiled and bowed, lifting his eyebrows a little in polite interrogation.

"Forgive me for being so forward, your Highness, but I and my friends are staunch supporters of the cause of freedom, and we would account it a great honour if you were able to join us at our table."

I saw the Russian's eyes flicker towards our group and his slight change in expression as he noted the beauty of Jane. He smiled, showing very white teeth. "The honour is mine, Mademoiselle," he said, with no more than a trace of accent. "May I know your name?"

"I am Cassandra Stevens and this is my sister Jane. With us also are two very stalwart comrades: Mr. Holmes and Dr. Watson."

We all rose and made our courtesies.

Our quarry seated himself and smiled all around. He ordered a liqueur and pressed by the girls, condescended to try one of the sandwiches cut to an almost impossible thinness for which the café is known.

"My sister and I are the publishers of the *Torch*," explained Cassandra, "a small periodical dedicated to encouraging rational debate on the inequality of our society, and we have followed your words and writings with the greatest interest."

"Indeed, I am aware of the fame of your excellent publication," lied our guest politely. "The cause is fortunate in having such talented and beautiful supporters."

We made conversation about the necessity and inevitability of social reform for some minutes. We then moved on to more personal matters as Prince Peter questioned and flattered the girls on their progress in the anarchist cause. The girls were excited and charmed by his manner. Jane seemed entranced by his royal rank and Cassandra by the depths of his commitment. Both I fear were fascinated and excited at the thought of the atrocities with which he was reputed to have be associated. I felt a burning within me that the finest specimens of English womanhood were in thrall to such a monster, but my role demanded that I conceal the emotion.

Although I said little, Holmes joined in the conversation and with his wide knowledge of many subjects including contemporary affairs was able to steer it to some extent. When at one point Cassandra mentioned some lectures which had moved her, Holmes was able in the most natural manner to refer to the weekly gatherings at the home of Ivan Koninski the famous Nihilist.

"Oh yes," breathed Jane. "Everybody has heard of those famous discussions. I would so like to attend but one must be invited and we have never met anyone who is of his circle."

"Perhaps Prince Peter might be able to introduce us?" said Holmes with a bow towards our guest.

Kropotkin said nothing immediately. Perhaps in order to give himself time to think he produced a cigarette case and extracted one of the long brown Russian cigarettes he favoured. From another pocket he took a silver vesta case in the shape of a cylinder capped with a skull; the skull being set with tiny rubies for eyes. He withdrew a match and lit the cigarette.

"Alas, Madame," he said regretfully, addressing Jane. "I fear not at this time. I beg for your understanding but in the high matters in which we are concerned my comrades would not allow me to take the slightest risk. I cannot introduce you on such short acquaintance. I hope we can meet again and when we come to know each other better it will be my pleasure to escort you there personally. On this occasion I am staying in England for only a few days on a matter of business. Perhaps in January when I expect to return, I might be permitted to meet you again?"

He leaned back in his chair; took a deep breath of smoke and elegantly breathed it out. "I am compelled to be careful," he added languidly, giving Jane a smile from lips that seemed very red in his pale face. "Police spies are everywhere." His eyes did not waver towards Holmes or myself but I was convinced he was mocking us.

The girls breathed their agreement to his caution, while Holmes concealed his chagrin under a conventional remark of regret. Soon after the Russian took his leave of us, bowing low over our companions' hands. We saw the girls into a cab and began our walk back to Baker Street. My friend was in a foul mood at the waste of a week of our limited time. On arrival at our lodgings he said nothing but slumped in his armchair with a set expression on his face. I judged it best to leave him alone and went about my own affairs.

I saw little of Sherlock Holmes in the following days; I believe he was out in one or the other of his many disguises trying to collect information from servants and idlers. Then one evening I entered to find him standing with a letter in his hand. "A message has just arrived from the Foreign Office," he said grimly. "Our diplomat returns to London tomorrow. And most unfortunately I have to confess that I have failed. Kropotkin talks to everybody and says nothing. He goes everywhere and does nothing. I have not the slightest indication of his henchmen. Nor am I sanguine enough to believe that Lestrade and his officers can outwit such a man. I confess, Watson, I am in the lowest spirits. The damage to my reputation I could bear, but the concept that my country will bleed as a result of my inadequacy is something I cannot endure." He turned away from me; his head bowed.

"Come, Holmes," I said bluffly. I feared that in this mood he would resort again to his hypodermic needle and cocaine solution. "We have had a setback but we can try again."

My friend did not deign to answer. I attempted a pleasantry: "Miss Jane and Miss Cassandra were the most delightful of stalking-horses, but perhaps too lightweight for our quarry."

My innocent words had a dramatic effect. Sherlock Holmes whirled round to face me; a wild expression on his face. I was taken aback, but he began to speak swiftly and intensely: "You have hit it, Watson! A stalking-horse! An ancient trick whereby the hunter conceals himself behind a creature that his prey considers harmless. But here the positions are reversed: Prince Peter is the stalking-horse, and it is we that are being gulled!"

Seeing my look of bafflement, he explained his reasoning.

"The summoning of Kropotkin was a blind. The Russian is our stalking-horse: he makes a great show and all our attention is diverted to him. Meanwhile the actual assassins take care to have nothing to do with him. Indeed, both sides will do everything possible to avoid making even the most tenuous link. We must give the police their due – there was never any chance that the Prince could evade their dogged persistence. We have channelled all our resources into keeping the wrong man under observation. Now we must ask ourselves: who is the protagonist? We know at once he is a different sort of person from Kropotkin. He works in the shadows rather than attending fashionable restaurants. He shuns company rather than holding forth at meetings.

"I think we can find a lead. I must send a message at once to the Foreign Office." Hastily, he scribbled a note while I summoned a messenger who was directed to take it to Lord Hawkesbury's secretary and wait for an answer. Holmes fumed impatiently until the reply arrived, although in fact it was less than an hour in arriving – a remarkable speed for a response from a government official. My friend swiftly scanned the missive.

"Come Watson: it is time that we paid another visit to Inspector Lestrade and confess our conversion to his views."

At Lestrade's office we were informed that he was patrolling with some of his men in Villiers Street, a short distance from the Savoy. We hurried to the spot and found him talking to three of his constables.

"Lestrade," said my friend, "I believe with you that Prince Peter is not an anarchist. I have come to ask humbly for your help. I need someone who can identify an anarchist or a sympathiser from a description."

Lestrade laughed in great good humour. "I thought you'd need police information sooner or later, Mr. Holmes. Well, I'm glad to give you a helping hand seeing as you've given me a hint or two in the past. Constable Blewitt here is with the Special Branch and knows all the anarchists."

Blewitt, a stolid man, nodded his head. "Yes, sir, that's right. Over the years you get to know them and their ways and the people they meet."

"I have here," said Sherlock Holmes, "the words of a report from the French authorities regarding a mysterious visitor from England. He stayed at a boarding house where the keeper is in the pay of the police. The informant says that the man could only manage a few words of French which he spoke in an accent that the keeper believed to be Russian. They communicated in English, in which language the man appeared to be at ease. This is significant as all Russian aristocrats speak French and we may therefore deduce that our man was not of the upper classes. He wore a coat trimmed with astrakhan fur – popular with the middle classes in Russia who cannot afford genuine fur. He is in late middle age, short in stature and with a neatly trimmed goatee beard. He is beginning to go bald at the back of the head and wears a cap to conceal it. He had some faint stains of ink on his hands which might well indicate a clerical profession."

The constable looked thoughtfully into the distance and rocked on his heels for a time. "That's a good description, sir. It might fit several of the men we know, but I would say it was Mr. Gogol. He's a bit vain about his appearance so he wears good clothes and he likes to cover his bald patch. He's been in this country for years and he speaks the language well."

"And where is he now?"

The constable shook his head. "He used to lodge in Battersea but I haven't seen him about there recently. We

139

don't see much of him at any time to tell the truth. He's a close man he is and very glum. He doesn't mix with the others much. I heard that his wife died of starvation in a Russian prison and since then he's hated any sort of authority. One thing I'll say for him; he's not work-shy: he gets regular jobs translating documents for firms that have business in Russia."

Suddenly Lord Hawkesbury's words to us flashed through my mind: *we have had to employ three extra clerk translators.* "Holmes!" I gasped. But my friend was already sprinting towards the Strand. "The Foreign Office!" he shouted to Lestrade over his shoulder. "Follow us as quickly as you can! It's life or death!"

Sherlock Holmes ran out into the street and waved his arms at a cab that was approaching at a sharp trot. He narrowly avoided being run down. "The Foreign Office!" he shouted. "Two sovereigns if you get us there in five minutes!"

Fortunately the cabman was a young and alert young fellow who whipped up his horse with no further words. We turned corners dangerously but to my relief soon saw our destination in the distance. Holmes flung the sovereigns at the cabbie and dashed up the steps of the Foreign Office.

"Do you have a clerk translator named Mr. Gogol?" he demanded of the doorman. "We need to be taken to his office immediately!"

The doorman merely smiled gently. He was well used to people arriving in great haste and insisting on immediate attention. His response was to reach for his pen and a piece of paper. "Well sir, perhaps we do and perhaps we don't. If you could help me fill in this form with your details and your business, I'll see that it gets taken to the person responsible. May we start with your names and addresses gentlemen?"

At that moment, Lestrade and his officers came running into the entrance hall. "What's all this commotion –" began the doorman, before Lestrade seized him by the collar.

"That's enough of that my lad," he snarled. "Give this gentleman what he wants and be quick about it or I'll have you arrested."

The doorman looked outraged and began to protest until he became aware of the uniformed officers looking grimly at him. He pulled himself together and beckoned to a page.

"Show these gentlemen to Mr. Gogol's office, Perkins," he said, with what dignity he could muster.

"Come on son," said Lestrade to the page. "At the double; we're in a hurry!"

Nothing loath, the young man leapt up the stairs with all of us in hot pursuit. At the first floor he turned left and hared off down the corridor. We kept up as best we could and finally all piled into a dingy office piled with papers. In one corner was a sizeable deal box secured with a large padlock.

"What's this?" rapped Holmes, indicating the box.

"It arrived for Mr. Gogol yesterday," said the lad pertly. "Full of books and papers he needs for his work. Very heavy it is – it took four men to carry it up here. He kept telling them to be careful."

Holmes grabbed a poker from the fireplace and inserted it under the padlock. With a wrench the hasp tore out of the wood and my friend flung up the lid.

Before us we saw an infernal machine. The box was three-quarters filled with a pile of powder the colour of dirty chalk. A cheap carriage clock was laying face-down on the powder. Holmes gently prised open the circular door on its back. Tied to the striking hammer was a small packet of linen. "The detonator," murmured Holmes as he carefully grasped the hammer at its pivot and twisted it out of position. "Mercury fulminate or some such substance. There: it is safe!"

The foreign diplomat returned to London the next day and completed his task without incident. The matter of the African colonies was resolved to the satisfaction of all parties. The police searched for the dynamitard Gogol at his

141

known haunts but with no success. Prince Peter returned to Paris the day after our discovery. There was of course no action that could be taken against him. Lord Hawkesbury sent for Holmes to thank him personally, and again emphasised the need for absolute secrecy in the national interest. He was successful in his aim as no hint of the attempted outrage came to public knowledge.

I found it significant however that in the following months an Aliens Bill was introduced to give the authorities powers to quiz immigrants to Great Britain, before indeed they were even allowed to disembark from their ship. In presenting the bill to the House, the Foreign Secretary was eloquent in a speech in which he said that our noted tolerance had done nothing but make us a haven for malcontents and murderers that held our ideals in contempt even as they benefited from our substance.

THE ADVENTURE OF THE EMINENT COLLECTOR

ERHAPS the most curious setting for the start of one of our adventures was the home of a famous collector of antiquities who lived in Bloomsbury, not far from the Museum. A note had been hand-delivered to Holmes asking him to present himself at Chenies Square that morning, but giving no hint of the purpose of the meeting. Holmes had asked if I would be interested in accompanying him and I had readily agreed: aside from the likely interest of a case, I had always wished to see something of the collection itself.

We strolled to the meeting place as it is not very distant from Baker Street, and found ourselves in a square of very tall but narrow houses built of brick blackened by two centuries of London grime. The footman that answered the door was swarthy of skin and with hawk-like features – I conjectured that he was of the Egyptian race. We were expected and he bowed us into the hall. Large as it was, it was dominated by a huge but crudely carved marble sarcophagus obviously of very great antiquity. Other pieces of sculpture were also crowded about, some on pedestals; some smaller pieces hanging on the walls but many simply standing on the floor, so that despite the size of the hall it was not easy to move about. I gazed about me in fascination.

We were conducted up to the first floor, and into a fine drawing room also lined with curios but here they were arranged on shelves and did not much intrude upon the room itself. In the main they seemed to be antique scientific instruments. I noted several astrolabes and a large and magnificent orrery. The broad windows of the room commanded a fine view over the gardens of the square.

In a chair in the centre of this room sat an old man in rich but shabby clothing. His expression was glowering. This

143

was clearly our client. Beside him sat a beautiful young woman with blonde hair. She wore an indoor gown of a dark brown colour. I tentatively deduced that she was a daughter of the house. The servant bowed to his employer.

"Misters Harms and Wa'son," he uttered.

The old man did not rise. "Be seated, gentleman," he said shortly, gesturing to chairs a short distance away.

As the servant made no move to help, we were obliged to move the chairs ourselves to convenient positions before we could comply with his instructions.

"It is in fact *Doctor* Watson," I ventured.

"No doubt it is," replied the old gentleman testily. "I am Sir Simon Hardwick, and I have summoned you here on a most serious matter."

"If you would be so kind as to outline the problem?" requested Holmes coolly.

"I have been robbed, Mr. Holmes," was the snarled response. "Robbed of an invaluable manuscript which would have revolutionised our view of a period of British history."

"Dear me," murmured my companion, "please give me more details."

"It is a parchment letter dated 1586 from William Maitland of Lethington, principal Secretary of State in the reign of Mary, Queen of Scots. It was stolen from my agent in a violent attack."

The young lady intervened here, "Perhaps we should explain, Sir Simon, that your agent Signor Ladrazzo is commissioned to bring you any manuscripts that he believes might interest you. He has recently brought a series of letters from Maitland, and yesterday evening was his latest offering. He was assaulted and the item stolen."

Holmes pursed his lips. "So the letter is not strictly speaking your property?" he asked.

"It is Ladrazzo's property that he was bringing to sell to me," snapped Sir Simon impatiently. "The exact legal position need not concern you."

"Very well," said my friend. "Where and when did the assault occur?"

"Directly outside my own house! The taxes we pay to maintain a police service are a fraud on the public, sir. As for the time, it was about eight o'clock in the evening. Miss Latimer here" – he gestured at the young lady – "was the first on the scene."

Miss Latimer, who I now realised was our client's assistant rather than a relative, again took up the tale. "I heard the doorbell ring yesterday evening: it was dark of course at this time of year. As we were expecting Signor Ladrazzo I opened the door myself. To my horror I found the gentleman with blood streaming down his forehead. I took him at once to the housekeeper's room and tended to him. He had a large contusion on the rear of his head and the skin was broken. He told me that as he was approaching our door, an assailant had struck him from behind and as he lay stunned, rummaged through his pockets and stole the letter."

"How valuable would the letter be?" asked Holmes.

"In the sphere of history, it is priceless," Sir Simon said emphatically. "I will pay you a considerable sum for its return. In terms of monetary worth," he went on less vehemently, "I am able to pay my agent five pounds per letter."

Holmes made a *moue*. "The theft seems to have been a hazardous proceeding for such a sum," he said. "What did the letter say?"

"I've no idea," sneered Sir Simon, "because it was stolen before I took possession of it."

"Quite so," responded my friend calmly, "but you must obviously have some inkling of its contents because of your statement that it would alter our view of history."

"Yes, very well," grumbled Sir Simon. "The letter was one of a series that have come into my hands and therefore we can guess at its subject. You will recall that in 1585 Mary, Queen of Scots was imprisoned in Carlisle Castle. Maitland has always been supposed to be unswervingly loyal to his

145

queen, but these letters to Baron Burghley indicate that as Mary's position became worse, he was trying to ingratiate himself with the English throne. It may well be that in later correspondence he betrayed the existence of the Anthony Babington plot to execute Queen Elizabeth, so leading Mary to the headsman's block!"

Holmes did not actually shrug; no doubt because such an action would have aroused his client's fury. "The letter is clearly of great historical interest," he conceded, "but I am puzzled by several matters. Firstly that someone should be such an enthusiast for the period that he would actually organise an assault to possess the letter. Do you know of anyone who has such an extreme interest in Elizabethan times that he would countenance such an attack?"

"I most certainly do," spat Sir Simon, "that charlatan in Dulwich who imagines he is a scholar when in fact he is a dilettante, sir, a mere dilettante."

"Ah, yes," mused Holmes. "I believe I have heard of the gentleman to whom you refer."

"Who has not? The man fills his home with mummified bodies, shrunken heads and stuffed animals. He has made himself notorious with the ignorant public and a laughing-stock with all serious antiquaries. His wealth – derived from the grocery trade I might say – has made it possible for this dabbler to deprive serious collectors such as myself of many important items. He is completely unprincipled. Now it seems he stoops to instructing thugs to steal items he cannot buy."

"Well, we must certainly consider that possibility," allowed Sherlock Holmes. "It seems to me also that the assailant was either remarkably lucky, or had foreknowledge that your agent was carrying important documents of the Elizabethan period. With whom else have you discussed the matter?"

Sir Simon and Miss Latimer looked at one another. "Well, I believe we did mention it to Herr Schuldig," she ventured. "Sir Simon has engaged the Siemens Company to install electric current in the house and Herr Schuldig is overseeing the work. He is a regular visitor – in fact he is here at the moment. He is a cultured man and has shown interest in our collection. Apart from him, the other residents are servants."

"May I take this opportunity to speak to the gentleman?" asked my friend.

Sir Simon rang the bell for a footman and shortly afterwards Schuldig was presented to us. My first impressions were not favourable. He was a fleshy man with a double chin and an unpleasant sheen to his skin. He smiled obsequiously at us, clasping his hands together.

"Good morning," said Sherlock Holmes. "I understand it is your responsibility to bring the advantages of electric light to these premises?"

"Yess, indeed. It is a great privilege, and a great benefit to every educated man. The gas fumes you understand, they give out smoke with sulphur in it and much water – much more water than one knows – this will attack Sir Simon's vonderful books. And of course, always the danger of fire. The electrical way is the best."

"I agree completely: electricity is a great boon. Now, you will have heard of the recent attack and robbery. I understand you were not in the house at the time?"

"No, I left this house at about six o'clock. I was in my lodgings at the time of the attack. So unfortunately I can tell you nothing."

"Are you acquainted with the victim?"

Schuldig seemed to hesitate slightly. "No," he said at last. "I never meet him. I only hear of him from Sir Simon and Miss Latimer."

"Have you mentioned him to anyone else?"

"No, no. It is not my concern. I am here only for the electric."

"I see," said Holmes dryly. "Thank you for your assistance."

When Schuldig had been dismissed, Holmes turned again to the client. "It is possible that Signor Ladrazzo himself boasted of his discovery, or the person which whom he deals may have been indiscreet, although in my experience such people are close-mouthed about their activities. I will speak to Ladrazzo and see what light he can throw on the matter. In the meantime I believe I have the information I need to start my investigation, but may I ask you to lend me the last two letters of the series so that I may have them examined?"

Sir Simon gestured at Miss Latimer who arose gracefully and walked to a fine writing desk veneered in black walnut. She unlocked a drawer and produced two sheets of folded parchment which she brought over to my friend.

"Written in French I see," was his comment on first inspection.

"Yes, Mr. Holmes," said the girl. "Middle French in fact, as written and spoken between the 14th and 16th centuries. The upper classes in Tudor times often wrote in French."

"I take it you are conversant with Middle French?"

"Certainly. I studied mediæval and Elizabethan history at University College."

I must confess that I was most taken by this combination of beauty and learning. She seemed to me to epitomise Tennyson's famous lauding of 'sweet girl-graduates in their golden hair'.

"Miss Latimer is invaluable to me," acknowledged Sir Simon. "She is currently engaged in cataloguing bundles of Elizabethan documents that I have bought at auction."

Holmes rose. "We wish you good day, sir," he said, "and we will bring you a report as soon as may be."

"Do we first visit the Italian?" I suggested as we left the house.

"Not at the moment, Watson. You have often in your writings deplored my cynical nature. I fear my current actions will not cause you to revise your opinions. We will first go to a person I know of to test the authenticity of these documents."

"You believe they are forged?"

"Given the nebulous state of this entire affair, I believe it to be highly likely. Let us at least test this theory and if it is proved, why then our client has no reason to worry about the loss of the manuscript but only of recovering his money from a scoundrel."

Holmes led me to a dingy antiquarian bookshop in Pied Bull Yard, which is very close to the Museum. Entering and weaving our way though piles of dusty volumes we found a small alcove at the back where sat a wizened creature. He looked up as we approached, and smiled uneasily, "Why, Mr. Holmes! What an honour that you should visit my premises."

"Good morning Franklin," said Holmes, "I have come into possession of these pieces of parchment and wonder if you would be so good as to give me your opinion of their provenance."

Franklin accepted the documents wordlessly and took them over to the window. He seemed to read each through carefully. Then screwing a jewellers' loupe into his eye he scanned the parchment at a very close distance; first checking over the surface, then turning it to the light and going over it again. Stepping back to his desk he picked up a fine scalpel of the kind surgeons use for the most delicate operations and scratched at the ink. In the end he shrugged.

"My opinion is that they are genuine, Mr Holmes. If you would care to leave the documents I could apply further tests, but I doubt that I will change my mind."

"They could not perhaps be palimpsests?"

"That is one of the first things I look for. One of the most common tricks is to get a piece of worthless parchment – perhaps an old land deed – and scrape off the writing. But the erasure always leaves traces. The surface of the skin will be covered with tiny scores and in addition there will almost always be traces of the original text. There is no sign of these so I conclude the parchment was blank before writing.

"Then we turn to the ink. You must understand sirs," he continued in a didactic tone, "that in matters of this sort it is important to confer age from the start, not attempt to add it afterwards. So for instance you would prepare ink as our ancestors did from oak galls and gum arabic, but you must then dilute it before you use it so that it gives a faded appearance, not try to bleach it after the writing is complete. Even when this is done, your newly-made ink will stick well to the parchment. Here I see that the ink is dry and powdery and does not adhere well; it is undoubtedly of some considerable age. In sum, I take your letters to be genuine examples of the period."

Holmes nodded and picked up the parchments. "Thank you Franklin," he said in what struck me as a rather pointed manner. "You have done me a valuable service." The man smiled grimly in response.

As we left my friend explained their relationship. "Franklin is a poacher turned gamekeeper, Watson. He once forged a will so skilfully it deceived me for some little time. It seemed to me that one with such valuable skills should not languish in gaol when I had a use for him. I therefore turned the man that had ordered the forgery over to the police and tipped the wink to Franklin, while making it quite clear that any repetition would be his downfall. In return he helps me with problems such as this. He currently makes a living restoring volumes. If some of the restoration is, shall we say, a little imaginative, I do not believe that any great harm has been done.

"But back to the matter at hand. The case grows interesting. It appears the manuscripts are exactly what they seem. Therefore we may suppose the attack was genuine. Let us now repair to the British Museum library, which is close at hand and get an expert opinion on the contents of our letters."

The Museum was only across the street from Franklin's premises. Holmes led the way through the great halls to where the Reading Room sits at the very centre. As always I was awed by its great size and the enormous glass dome high overhead. I was aware that Holmes held a Readers' ticket and often used the library for background research when his own more contemporary index failed him.

At the desk Holmes asked for Professor Gray. This gentleman arrived shortly and shook my friend's hand warmly. "Good morning, Mr. Holmes! What can I do for you today?" he asked. He was a cheerful-looking, rather elderly man. He conformed to the stock image of a professor by sporting a full beard and wearing a tweed suit.

"Good morning, Professor! I have been entrusted with these parchment letters, which purport to be from William Maitland of Lethington. I would be infinitely obliged for your opinion on their contents."

Professor Gray accepted the letters and read through them. "Hum, most interesting!" was his comment at last. "You may be aware that for his deviousness William Maitland was nicknamed 'Michael Wily': a felicitous play on the name of Machiavelli. He was involved in the conspiracy to murder David Rizzio, private secretary and rumoured lover of Queen Mary. Despite this, he was able to regain the Queen's favour and later served in her government. At one time he was Mary's ambassador to England and would undoubtedly have made many acquaintances among the aristocracy. These letters seem to show that he was up to his old trick of running with the fox and hunting with the hounds."

As Holmes and the professor were talking I glanced aside and caught sight of a familiar profile hurrying past. "Why, Herr Schuldig!" I exclaimed, "What a surprise to see you here!"

Schuldig started and abruptly halted his progress. Turning to face me he recovered himself and gave an ingratiating smile. "Dr. Watson," he said, his plump cheeks shining with sweat, "it is a pleasure to see you again so soon!"

"You are here professionally?"

"Yess, yess, certainly! My company Siemens also the electricity for this library supplies. The most vonderful collection in the world. It is a great honour. But if you will excuse me, I must be about my work: in this large building there is much to do."

"Of course."

Holmes had taken note of our exchange. "We met Herr Schuldig earlier today at the home of another of his clients," he said casually to the professor when the German had hurried off. "He appears to know his business well."

"Certainly: an invaluable man! You would perhaps not recall Mr. Holmes, but ten years ago this library was a dark and gloomy place. With only a large gas lantern burning under the dome we were unable to work on dark and foggy days. And of course there was always the terror of fire which would have caused unthinkable harm to scholarship.

"Happily, that is all now in the past. The electric ray allows us to work what hours we please, unburdened by restrictions of climate or season. Strangely enough, the only complaint we have had is that the light is too white for readers accustomed to gaslight!"

"The grooves of change, as the poet has it, will sometimes chafe for a while," remarked Sherlock Holmes. "Please accept my sincere thanks for giving us this assistance. Your erudition has as always been most enlightening."

"Are you pressed for time? Because if not I would greatly welcome the opportunity to make transcripts of these letters. If there is no objection of course."

"I cannot imagine that my client would object in the least," said Holmes urbanely. I was less sanguine regarding Sir Simon's possessiveness towards his manuscripts, but said nothing.

While Professor Gray was making his copies Holmes and I sat on one of the leather benches which radiate out from the central dais talking in low voices so as not to disturb the other readers in the great room.

"Have you reached any conclusions?" I asked.

"The motive for the theft continues to elude me," complained my friend. "If the assailant wanted a relatively small sum of money, why did he not simply rob a rich drunkard in a dark street in Soho and take his pocket-book? There must exist here a great desire for that particular letter, but there surely cannot be such extreme interest in manuscripts of the Elizabethan period that were not actually written by one of the monarchs of the time."

"Perhaps it is what is written on the parchment that makes it so important," I suggested. "If the lost letter perhaps revealed some dishonourable act done by a noble person of the time a descendant might be anxious to protect the name of his family at any cost."

"After four hundred years? I doubt it. Even the most outrageous scandal acquires a patina of romance after so long a time. The Duke of St. Albans sits in the House of Lords and does not feel that his dignity is impaired by being descended from the lovely but wanton Nell Gwynne."

"What about Sir Simon's theory that the rival collector in Dulwich is involved?"

"I do not take that seriously, Watson. The collecting mania takes different men in different forms. The Dulwich collector's interest is mainly anthropological: he values the fantastic and the exotic. I doubt he would be interested in a piece of Elizabethan parchment whatever was written on it. Besides, unscrupulous as collectors are in pursuit of their prey, I also doubt that he would go as far as to have it stolen.

"I suspect that the most likely motive is that the letter has been held for ransom and Sir Simon will shortly receive a demand for a large sum, probably combined with the threat of destroying the letter if payment is not made. If so, we can see that it was not simply an opportunistic theft: the villain knew very well what he was about and is conversant with the typical mania of collectors, where they will pay almost anything to complete a series."

After about twenty minutes Professor Gray returned with our originals. Thanks were exchanged on all sides and we found ourselves once more in the wide courtyard of the Museum.

"I believe we have time to visit the Italian before we take our tea," said Holmes. He raised his stick and hailed a hansom. "Saffron Hill!" he called to the cabman.

The hansom took us to Saffron Hill; the long, narrow and squalid thoroughfare that separates Holborn and Clerkenwell. In recent years it has become the home of the Italian race. Organ grinders, ice-cream sellers, musicians, artists; all the professions which the Italians have made their own have clustered in this street.

We alighted at a doorway peeling with old paint and knocked. A young woman answered. She looked at us with suspicion in which a good deal of fear was intermingled. "Signor Ladrazzo?" we enquired. She did not reply, perhaps not speaking English, or speaking it imperfectly, but obviously recognised the name as she went to the foot of the stairs and called: "Luigi!"

After a few moments a door opened and a young man walked down the stairs. He was handsome in the Italian manner, with the head of a young David and tight curls.

He looked at us suspiciously.

Holmes bowed. "Signor Ladrazzo I take it?" he said. "We have been retained by Sir Simon Hardwick to look into the matter of the theft of his letter. May we come in and ask you a few questions?"

The Italian looked as if he would like to refuse this request, but did not dare. "Come into my room," he said grudgingly, turning and leading the way.

Climbing the bare and dirty wood of the stairs we came to a room on the first floor. Ladrazzo indicated a shabby settee on which we sat, while he took a seat on his bed. The room was sordid and cluttered to the last degree. There however some marks of scholarship, or at least of antiquarian dealing, in the piles of leather-bound books and sheaves of parchments that stood on every flat surface.

"Can I first ask you, signor," said Sherlock Holmes, "when you first began working for Sir Simon?"

"Perhaps since a year."

"Always Elizabethan manuscripts?"

"No. At the beginning I brought him some incunabula. Old prayer books from Germany."

"And when did you offer the series of Elizabethan letters?"

Ladrazzo paused in thought. "January," he said finally.

"About three months ago then?"

"Yes."

"And what was the source of these documents?"

The Italian looked cunning. "If I tell you, maybe you get the letters yourself and take my business. It is a secret."

"You have told no-one else then about the existence of the letters?"

"No. I keep it all a secret."

"The person who robbed you knew you were carrying a valuable letter and knew the time you were expected in Chenies Square. Who could that have been?"

Ladrazzo shrugged. "How should I know? Maybe the woman: Miss Latimer. The women are for ever talking."

"Both she and Sir Simon claim to have told no-one."

"Then I don't know," said the Italian mulishly.

Holmes persisted with more questions, but it was clear that we were going to get nothing of significance from the man. Finally my friend rose and bowed.

"Thank you for your assistance, Signor Ladrazzo. I hope we will not need to trouble you again and I can assure you that I will make every effort to bring the villain that assaulted you to justice."

Perhaps it was my imagination, but I seemed to see a flicker of unease cross the face of the young man.

Leaving the house, we strolled towards Clerkenwell Road in search of a cab. "We have earned our tea, Watson," remarked my friend. "Let us return to Baker Street to see what Mrs. Hudson can offer us."

Early next morning we received another peremptory summons from Sir Simon. In it he stated that he had received a demand for payment for return of the stolen letter.

155

Holmes looked pleased. "It is as I predicted, Watson. The letter is being held for ransom. This may open the case for us. There is much to be learned from any missive and the process of exchanging money for the purloined items gives many opportunities to seize the rascal. Let us be off!"

On our arrival the servant that opened the door informed us that Sir Simon was in his study and wished us to join him there. We followed the man up the stairs, this time to the second floor. At the landing the way led through an arched opening gated with an ornate metal grille that had once guarded the entrance to the seraglio of a great Caliph. I was a few moments ahead of Holmes who had paused to study some Hogarth engravings that hung up the stairway.

As I followed the footman through the arch, which was rather narrow, my hand brushed against the grille. Immediately I felt a dreadful ache shoot through my bones then a burning pain as my hand involuntarily clenched and clasped the metal. I tried to twist myself aside but my muscles would not obey me. My body began to spasm. I tried to shout but could only make a croaking noise. A more violent convulsion brought me into contact with a pedestal. I knocked heavily against it and was aware of the statue placed on top beginning to fall. It toppled and the weight of the marble threw me backwards on to the rug. In falling, my grasp on the grille was broken and the ache immediately lessened although I felt badly bruised.

I heard steps pounding up the stairs and abruptly Holmes was there. "Watson!" he cried kneeling down and bending over me. "What in heaven's name has happened!"

I was not able to speak, but pointed wordlessly to the electric light above us and then to the grille. Holmes realised immediately what I was trying to say.

"Electricity!" he muttered. Steps sounded from the other direction as Sir Simon also came investigating the source of the disturbance. He reached us at his slower pace and observed the scene. His features distorted with shock and dismay.

"My Venus!" he cried pitifully. "Is she damaged?" He rushed to the fallen statue and knelt at its side to inspect it closely. "No, no, it is well!" he said at last. "You are unbroken my lovely, not even a tiny chip. The rug saved you, eh? Well done!" He stroked the white marble almost lasciviously.

Holmes looked at him with distaste. "Watson has suffered an electrical shock, Sir Simon. Touch nothing metal. Where is Herr Schuldig?"

"He was here a short while ago," said Sir Simon, looking up. "I believe he is testing a new lighting system in the blue drawing room."

"Would you have the goodness to send for him?"

In a few minutes Schuldig arrived. By then I had the strength to sit up. "Herr Schuldig," said Holmes grimly, "Watson has suffered an electrical shock from this grille. I believe this falls into your purview?"

"Ah yes! I see. Most unfortunate!" said the German abjectly. "I beg you all to stand exactly where you are and I will the current disconnect." He hurried off on his errand.

"How can we help you, old friend?" asked Sherlock Holmes.

"Just leave me a while, Holmes. The electrical pain will pass away with a little time. Apart from that I think I have only minor bruising and this burn on my palm."

Schuldig returned soon afterwards. Holmes turned to him and said, "Would you have the goodness to check and see how this could have happened, Herr Schuldig? The results could have been most unfortunate."

"Yess, off course. At once!" said the German. "It must be the new wiring. Yes! See here the covering on the wire to this light has been worn away where it passes over the railing. This made the metal live. Ferry unfortunate. I cannot imagine how it happened."

"Indeed!" said Holmes, distrust in every syllable. He bent and looked at the wire, fingering it a while and twisting it in his hands. "Hum! Best have it repaired at once. Come,

157

Doctor. If you are well enough to stand I will assist you back to our rooms where you can recuperate."

"Do you suspect foul play Holmes?" I murmured quietly as he helped me down the stairs.

"Perhaps," replied Homes, also in low tones. "If so it was skilfully done. The wire covering appears to have been abraded and is worn exactly at the point where it passes over the rail. The footman was largely protected as he wears gloves. The person who set the trap knew the ways of the electric current."

"Schuldig, then?" I asked.

"It seems the most likely conclusion. The trap was undoubtedly set for me. For a matter concerning an old piece of parchment, the risks seem disproportionate! But come; let us go home to Baker Street. You will be able put your feet up and Mrs. Hudson will make us both a cup of tea."

We took a hansom back, and there my friend made me comfortable while he went to attend to the matter of tea. On his return he flung himself into his favourite armchair, filled his pipe and meditatively blew smoke.

"We have come a great distance Watson, in the last twenty years," he mused. "When I read Natural Sciences at Cambridge in the 'seventies the subject of the electric current was barely mentioned. There was very little use of the phenomenon outside the laboratory, as practical generators had only just been invented. Now of course we see its benefits everywhere and as you have just found out, some of its drawbacks as well!"

He fell into a reverie, sitting silently as he considered all aspects of the problem. I knew his habits too well to think of disturbing him and engaged myself with my tea and the daily paper, taking care not to rustle the pages as I turned them. I am not sure how much time passed – I may have dozed off for a while after the exertions of the morning. I came to myself as my companion sprang to his feet with an exclamation.

Holmes walked swiftly over to the bookcases, as he often did when he wished to check a fact or research a subject. To my surprise however, rather than take a volume from his own sizeable collection, he went to the shelf that contained my scant row of medical texts. He selected a treatise on the integumentary system and settled down again to leaf through it. After perhaps ten minutes he threw down the book and turned to me.

"Are you recovered, Watson?"

"Yes, completely, thank you. Do you plan to go out again?"

"I plan to return to Chenies Square, Doctor! I have a vital question to put to Sir Simon!"

We hurried back to the client's house and were quickly shown into his presence. Holmes wasted no time with preliminary remarks. "Sir Simon," he said, "were you present when Miss Latimer was treating Signor Ladrazzo?"

"For much of the time, yes, I was. I heard the commotion and followed them to the housekeeper's room where she was treating the unfortunate young man."

"And did you observe if there was much blood?"

"Why, no. I recollect clearly that I was worried for the safety of one of my Persian rugs and was about to instruct a servant to move it, but I saw there was no need as only a very small amount of blood was present."

"Excellent!" said Holmes to my bemusement. "Will you be so good as to send a messenger to Signor Ladrazzo to ask him to come immediately? I believe that with his help we may be able to clear this matter up. And perhaps it would also be as well to send for Miss Latimer: I believe she also may be able to assist us."

Sir Simon gave the instructions, and we waited for the best part of an hour for the man to arrive. During that time we all pressed Sherlock Holmes for more details of his reasoning, but he refused to elaborate – if my friend had a weakness it was that he greatly loved the drama of a *dénouement.*

At last the Italian, surly and suspicious, was shown in. "Signor Ladrazzo!" cried Holmes springing to his feet in exuberant greeting. "I am very pleased to see you. May I ask you to kneel down?"

Ladrazzo stepped back at this: his face twisting into angry bafflement.

Holmes merely smiled and swiftly strode up to him. He grasped the Italian's arm and with his great strength twisted it and forced the man to his knees. Ladrazzo cried out in pain and fury. Sir Simon stood up, but was too confused to make any protest.

"Now Watson," said Holmes, maintaining his grip, "would you be so good as to inspect the wound?"

I knelt beside the man. Ladrazzo struggled but was gripped firmly. I parted his hair which was the characteristic thick and bushy mop of the Mediterranean races. I checked carefully over the scalp then looked up in astonishment.

"There is nothing, Holmes. I can find no lacerations at all; but even a surface injury could not possibly have healed in such a short time!"

"There never was a wound! As is typical of the southern races he was too cowardly to injure himself for the charade. What did you use Signor Ladrazzo – a piece of bloody steak perhaps? Squeezed over your head just before you knocked on the door?"

He released the Italian who sprang to his feet and stood with his fists clenched, trembling with anger.

"When Sir Simon told us there was little blood I guessed we would find this. A scalp wound bleeds copiously – is that not so Doctor? – because the scalp has a rich blood supply and its blood vessels do not constrict as they do in other parts of the body.

"And of course," continued Sherlock Holmes, turning abruptly to face Miss Latimer, who sat frozen and white-faced, "this discovery immediately indicts your assistant. She was working in collusion with the Italian.

'HE FORCED THE MAN TO HIS KNEES'

"Well, madam?" he said coldly, when she made no response. "Do you have nothing to say?"

She remained silent and Holmes turned to Sir Simon. "I believe you will find sir, that the letters you have purchased from Ladrazzo came from one of the bundles you yourself bought at auction. In her cataloguing duties Miss Latimer found a series of Elizabethan letters of the period that interests you. Rather than draw them to your attention she colluded with the Italian to defraud you.

"It is clear that they have been lovers for some time. She is after all not the first young woman to fall for continental good looks and overt passion. The scheme went well enough for a while, but they decided that five pounds per letter was not enough. There was no-one else in the market at that price so they decided to fake an assault, hoping that the natural desire of a collector to complete a series would enable them to demand a sizeable sum for its return.

"After my questioning of him, Ladrazzo decided that I was a danger to him and resolved to eliminate me. He hit on the idea of using the installation of electric current as a cover for his scheme. Let us not forget that electricity is an Italian discovery. Our friend seems versatile in his dealings and not unintelligent. I wonder if he might at some time in his native land have studied under the disciples of Galvani and Professor Volta? I conjecture that Miss Latimer smuggled him in at some time today when the front of the house was quiet; perhaps while breakfast was being served. He set the trap and then arranged for the ransom demand to be delivered, knowing that I would be summoned immediately.

"And now Sir Simon, if you would send one of your servants to the nearest police station we can have this pair arrested on charges of theft and fraud."

Our client seemed shocked by these revelations. He made no reply to my companion's suggestion, but merely stared at the floor while slowly shaking his head. After a time he raised his gaze to the guilty pair.

"Go!" he said fiercely. "Go now, and never let me set eyes on you again!"

Ladrazzo turned and hurried to the door at once. Miss Latimer followed him with alacrity. Clearly they were going to take immediate advantage of Sir Simon's generosity.

Holmes turned to him with raised eyebrows. "If you do not wish to press charges, sir, there is nothing I can do. I have to say however that you are making a mistake in letting such arrant rogues go free."

Sir Simon seemed suddenly old and shrunken. "They were my friends Mr. Holmes," he said sadly. "My fellow enthusiasts. I never thought they would betray me as they have done. Send in your bill: I will not quibble; you have done what I asked.

"As for you Dr. Watson, you will oblige me by not adding this most painful episode to that collection of lurid tales with which you entertain the lowest class of readers. And now I must ask both of you to leave me."

I bowed my assent, and with my friend took leave of our client for the last time.

THE ADVENTURE OF THE PAWNBROKER'S WIFE

T was a warm day in early autumn and Sherlock Holmes and I were finishing our breakfast at our lodgings at 221B Baker Street.

"Upon my word Watson," remarked my friend, "but this is far too good a day to stay indoors. We shall take a walk in the Regent's park across the road and perhaps stroll around the lake and admire the flowers and the beauties of nature."

I was heartily concurring with this plan, when Mrs. Hudson came in to clear away the dishes and said to Holmes, "There is a young lady asking to see you sir, I told her you were at breakfast and asked her to wait in the parlour."

"Thank you Mrs. Hudson: a very energetic young lady to start the day so early. I doubt she is a lady of leisure."

When we met her, I saw that Holmes' guess had been right. She was neatly but plainly dressed. Her expression was serious, but not to my observation desperate. I noted she wore no wedding ring and surmised it might be an affair of the heart.

"Thank you for seeing me, sir," she began. "My name is Marie Franklin. I have come to see you because I am troubled in my mind with a problem – or it may be a very great coincidence – and I would greatly appreciate your advice."

"Tell me everything in the order it occurred,"said Holmes, throwing himself back in his chair and closing his eyes.

"Well sir, I must tell you first that my father is dead and I live with my mother and her second husband in Highgate. Next door to our home is a pawnbroker's run by a Mr. Sharpe. He and my stepfather are great friends and often drink together in the neighbouring hostelries.

"Two months ago, Mr. Sharpe's wife died quite suddenly of failure of the heart. She was not an old woman so it was something of a shock to me as we often met and spoke. It was especially so since her husband was away from home for a few days on business – something that has never happened before in my memory – and he found her dead on his return. I shudder, Mr. Holmes, to think of her lying there dead beyond the wall from my bedroom, and with no-one to claim her.

"After the funeral Mr. Sharpe did not seem much cast down. And in fact a short while later he began to pay attentions to me: attentions which I have to say I did not encourage. It may be very shallow of me, as he is no doubt an honest and hard-working man, but I find him repulsive in appearance and manner. At last he plucked up enough courage to inform me that he would like to make me his wife. I could hardly repress a shudder at the thought of sharing my life with him, but I told him that although I was grateful beyond measure for his offer I could not bring myself to love him. His only response was that perhaps he had spoken too soon and he would ask me again in a little while.

"My stepfather loses no opportunity to sketch the advantages of my becoming the pawnbroker's wife and living in some prosperity, rather than being the wife of a penniless young man where I would have to work much harder. All very true no doubt, but I am still not so minded. In fact, I suspect a less worthy motive for his concern: my late father left our cottage to myself, with the stipulation that it could not be sold while my mother lives. I suspect that my stepfather has come to an arrangement with Mr. Sharpe that he would be allowed to go on living there in the event of my marriage."

Still with his eyes closed Holmes put in a question: "Is there any doubt that the death was of natural causes?"

"No, sir, not exactly," said the lady after a short pause. "As she died suddenly there was a post-mortem. It was not carried out by her own doctor, for he was on holiday in northern France, but by a very reputable local man, Dr. Fletcher. The inquest brought in a verdict by death of failure of the heart."

My friend opened his eyes. "My dear young lady," he said, "I sympathise with your predicament, but what can a mere consulting detective do here? Mr. Sharpe is hardly the first older man to be attracted by a lady much younger than himself. And as a widower he is free to press his suit. You can always refuse him."

"There is the matter of the strange coincidence, Mr. Holmes. It often happens that the pawnbroker's clients cannot or do not redeem their pledges, and then after a period of time they are sold. One afternoon a week before she died, I saw the wife hanging out a handsome mourning suit to dry. We spoke over the garden wall and she told me that her husband had asked her to wash and press it to make it look at its best for a sale. The next time I saw that suit was on her husband standing at her graveside in Highgate cemetery. She had been preparing her own funeral clothes." Her face tightened with the horror of the recollection.

"It may of course be simply a macabre coincidence," mused Holmes, "but I think I will take your case Miss Franklin; it promises to have some points of interest. Watson and I were about to take a stroll in the Regent's park, but the fresh airs and elevated situation of Highgate will do as well or better. We will accompany you home if we may and look into the matter at its fount."

Within the hour we had arrived in Highgate. At Miss Franklin's request we stopped the cab in the High Street, she explaining that if her neighbours saw her alighting from a hackney it would certainly cause comment. We then walked down West Hill towards Parliament Hill Fields. On one of the steeply sloping streets of the village we came to Miss Franklin's home.

"I cannot ask you to come in sir," she apologised, "my stepfather would be angry with me at bringing outsiders into what he regards as his affairs."

"I understand. We will make our own investigations, and meet you later to discuss what might arise from them. Where would be convenient for that purpose?"

"Pritchett's coffee rooms in the High Street is a most respectable place," returned the girl.

"Eminently suitable. Shall we say then, in three hours time?"

The girl left us, and Holmes said, "The obvious starting place is the pawnbroker's. Let us go inside and see Mr. Sharpe for ourselves."

We entered into the dark shop. A musty smell hung around from the old clothes. Many of the poor people would pawn their overcoats in the summer and redeem them when the colder weather came. Numerous clocks and small ornaments were displayed on shelves well beyond the counter. A few musical instruments of the more portable kind such as fiddles and concertinas were also present. In a glass case I saw jewellery of the cheaper sort: opals, jet, amethyst, moonstones, malachite and other semi-precious stones. The pawnbroker himself came out of the rear of the shop. Seeing two men dressed better than the average he bowed, rubbing his hands. The obsequious smile on his face failed to disguise his obvious suspicion that we might be officialdom.

"Good morning gentlemen," he said, "what can I do for you today?"

"I am a collector of curiosities", said Holmes in an off-hand manner, "and I happened to be passing your shop and have called in to see what you might have of a general nature."

"I am always very happy to assist an antiquarian, being something of one myself sir," said the man fawningly. "Not a large stock of curiosities unfortunately in a place such as this; in some ways you might do better at Deptford or Greenwich where the sailors come. Still, I do have a few choice pieces that might appeal to a gentleman such as yourself. Over here, for instance, sir," he said, indicating a corner of the shop piled with a miscellany of items, "we have some very interesting articles that were collected by the late Colonel Thomas of Southwood House when he was stationed in South Africa with the Welch Guards. I was fortunate enough to be able to buy these when his effects were auctioned on his death.

"Please observe this chieftain's chair carved from solid ebony. Notice the weight and solidity of the item. It would grace any gentleman's dining room or study. Over here are some fetich idols also mainly of ebony." He indicated a few grotesquely carved and painted idols about two to three feet tall; their faces very thin and with exaggerated cheeks and lips. "Observe the primitive power of these objects, sir. Perhaps not entirely suited to a home where a woman presides, but they would look most striking in a bachelor apartment."

Holmes nodded, "And these?" he said indicating some weaponry nearby, also obviously of African provenance.

"Ah, yes, sir" said Sharpe, "a very fine set, also from Colonel Thomas' collection. A complete set of armour as worn by a Zulu warrior: see the assegai and the shield. In very good condition, sir, and of the finest workmanship."

Holmes nodded languidly, "They are indeed fine pieces, but I doubt that they would fit in with my current collection." He walked about the shop for a while, peering at certain items. From my knowledge of my friend I had no doubt he was collecting what clues he could of Mr. Sharpe's predilections and income. He put a question to the pawnbroker.

"I live about two miles away; if I wanted the chair delivered could it be arranged?"

"Oh certainly, sir," Sharpe said eagerly, for the chair was clearly an expensive item, "I have a very serviceable handcart for the larger items."

Holmes seemed ready to go. "Thank you for your time, Mr. Sharpe," he said courteously, "there are certainly some items here of interest. I will consider the matter."

The pawnbroker showed us out, and we walked back along the road. I could not contain my curiosity but said as soon as we were a safe distance away, "Well, Holmes, what did you discover?"

Holmes raised his eyebrows in amusement. "Very little concerning the matter in hand, Watson, although we could hardly speak to the man about his romantic inclinations. I did note a curious feature of the Zulu weaponry, however."

"Indeed?" I said doubtfully, "Which piece of it was amiss?"

"Rather ask which piece of it was missing. There was no knobkerrie. Used as the standard weapon after the great Chaka introduced it to his impis and made them the most feared on the Dark Continent. It would have been carried by every warrior and the Colonel would not have omitted it from his collection."

"But Mrs. Sharpe was not killed by a knobkerrie or any other instrument," I protested.

"True. Well perhaps it is of no importance, but it is rather strange all the same. Now I think our paths had best diverge here, Watson. I am going to make some enquiries, as casual as may be, about Mr. and Mrs. Sharpe, while you would very kindly oblige me by calling on your colleague, Dr. Fletcher."

"I have it Holmes!" I said excitedly. "The substitute doctor is on the point of retirement or perhaps a prey to drink – in any case not competent. Sharpe might reasonably have expected that some subtle device might set past him."

Holmes gave me what I imagined to be a sardonic smile. "A plausible theory, Watson: perhaps you will be so kind as to make a professional visit to the gentleman to test it."

I walked up the hill again and into Pond Square in the fashionable heart of the village. There in a handsome Georgian house I found the surgery of Dr. George Fletcher.

After presenting my card I was ushered into his presence. I found myself before a tall well-built man. His face showed obvious signs of good living, and he was somewhat beyond middle age, but my theory of drink or dissipation died on the spot.

"Ah, Dr. Watson," he said heartily, "I am always pleased to meet a colleague. Would you care for some tea while you state your business?"

I accepted and we exchanged polite remarks about the clement weather. At last the maid wheeled in the tea trolley and left us. I broached the matter of Mrs. Sharpe, presenting myself as a distant relative as an excuse for my interest.

"Ah yes," said Dr. Fletcher, "I remember the matter perfectly well. I did not know that lady, but Dr. Hugh Smith and myself have an arrangement by which we take on each other's duties around this time of year. He prefers to take his holidays in the early summer when it is cooler and I in the late, so it works very well. When I was called in, Mrs. Sharpe had been dead some days. Unfortunately her husband had been away on business, and found her dead on his return. A sad business and a sad shock for the poor man on his homecoming. I officially confirmed death and had her remains taken to the Royal Free Hospital for a post-mortem. I also attended the inquest and gave formal evidence, but the post-mortem was unequivocal – heart failure."

I asked for a few more medical details regarding the general state of Mrs. Sharpe's health. There had apparently been no previous signs such as palpitations or shortage of breath, but these are not invariably present in a case of heart disease. After some further polite exchanges I took my leave of the good doctor and walked back with a heavy heart to where I had arranged to meet my friend. It was clear to me that Miss Franklin, for whom I had already conceived some affection, was simply clutching at straws. I said as much to Holmes.

"I cannot agree, Watson," he said emphatically, "there are too many coincidences for my liking – consider: the lady dies when her husband is from home – but he has never left home before. She dies within the month of the year that her doctor spends abroad. Even a set of mourning clothes of the correct size is ready. No Watson, I am convinced it was foul play."

"But the inquest, Holmes," I protested, "it was quite clear. The doctor, whether he knew her or not, is an experienced professional man who could not have failed to notice evidence of foul play. A mere pawnbroker could not hope to fool the resources of modern forensic science – to which you have notably contributed yourself."

"You flatter me as always Watson. But come, it is time for our appointment with Miss Franklin at Pritchett's coffee rooms."

There we all took a table for lunch. The food was plain but well cooked. After we had ordered, Holmes said to Miss Franklin, "I would appreciate knowing more of the relationship of Mr. and Mrs. Sharpe. Were they a devoted couple?"

"I think not, Mr. Holmes, although I heard no quarrels. She treated him with some disdain and often complained that he was not as generous with her allowance as she would wish. She always wished to dress well and I think perhaps she considered a pawnbroker beneath her."

"Interesting. Tell me do you know the name of her dressmaker?"

"Certainly. She often mentioned her. It is Mrs. Eliza Mortimer who has a shop in the High Street a short way from where we are sitting."

"One further question," said Holmes, "Mr. Sharpe told me he has a handcart. Do you happen to know when it is kept?"

"Yes sir. It is stored in Townsend Yard in a stable belonging to the farrier. He often uses it for furniture and other heavy or bulky items to save the cost of a carter."

We talked of various matters over the meal, Miss Franklin confiding that she was hoping to get a situation with the Highgate and Hornsey building society, which had agreed to interview her for a vacancy.

We did not linger over the meal, for Holmes was anxious to follow up his investigations. We took our leave of the young lady, Holmes saying in parting, "I am still in the early stages of this case, Miss Franklin but I feel there may well be something I can do for you. I will contact you if I may, tomorrow."

She thanked us earnestly, pressing both our hands in farewell. We bowed our leave, then Holmes said, "Now Watson, we may find some useful information at the dressmaker's: let us go to Mrs. Mortimer's establishment."

We walked along the High Street and found the shop. Mrs. Mortimer herself came forward to meet us; a tall and haughty woman with, to my taste, an over-dramatic inclination in clothing and a complexion that owed more to artifice than to nature. She seemed at least content to receive gentlemen.

Holmes bowed. "Mrs. Mortimer? We represent the executors of the estate of the late Mrs. Dorothy Sharpe. We understand that there is an amount outstanding on her account."

Mrs. Mortimer unbent at once at this introduction, "Please come into my office, gentlemen, where we can discuss the matter in more comfort."

We entered her office, a cramped and untidy area. Obviously paperwork was not the lady's forte. Taking up most of the desk was a large accounts book. We seated ourselves, and by way of a preliminary Mrs. Mortimer clasped her hands and announced soulfully, "I was mortified to hear of her passing over. I regarded her not as a client, merely, but also as a dear friend. She was so young to be taken from her family and friends, but, alas, gentlemen, these matters are in the hands of an all-wise Providence!"

We murmured agreement, and with a heavy sigh Mrs. Mortimer turned her attention to the accounts book. After some little consultation she was able to tell us, "At her tragic death, Mrs. Sharpe's account stood at £3 2s 4d. That includes a new walking-out dress for the summer months, which she ordered and was fitted for, but of which she sadly never took delivery."

"May I see?" asked Holmes. She turned the book to us and Holmes gave it a careful inspection. I saw that well over a page was given up to a list of garments made. Knowing Holmes' methods as I did, I had no doubt he was taking the opportunity to view the entire history of the account.

"That seems perfectly in order, madam," he said finally. "Tell me, have you mentioned your account to Mr. Sharpe?"

Mrs. Mortimer pursed her lips: "I have indeed, sir, after of course waiting a suitable time after the funeral. Mr. Sharpe was most unhelpful: he stated that his wife had left many debts and he would have to consider the matter. Not only unbusiness-like, but also, in my opinion, disrespectful of his late wife."

Sherlock Holmes nodded sympathetically. "You will understand that we cannot disburse funds until we have a clear idea of everything that is due," he said. "However, I hope that in due course we will be able meet all that is owing." My friend took out his note-book and wrote down some particulars. He then rose, as did I and Mrs. Mortimer.

"Thank you for your trouble, Madam," he said politely. "We will be in touch shortly."

Mrs. Mortimer showed us out with a genteel smile.

"A sizeable account there, Holmes," I remarked, "and from what the lady said, Mrs. Sharpe has been free with her money elsewhere. She does appear to have been rather extravagant for a woman in her position; or do you rather suspect that the husband has funds which he takes care to keep concealed?"

"Let us not reason ahead of our data, my dear Watson," he reproved me. "But come, we have one more person to visit: Mrs. Sharpe herself!"

It was a short if steep downhill walk that led us to Swain's Lane and the entrances to Highgate cemetery, which the narrow road bisects. We entered and inquired of the custodian the way to Mrs. Sharpe's grave. He led us about half a mile into the grounds, where the more recent graves are situated. Our path took us through the cemetery and past a remarkable profusion of marble statuary. There were many examples of the traditional angels and broken columns but there were also more unusual shapes: a fireman's helmet for a brave man who gave his life in the course of his duties; a large marble piano over the grave of a pianist; several people had statues of their faithful dogs erected with them. The whole was clean and well weeded and well kept. Some tombs were almost as big as small houses in themselves.

We came at last to Mrs. Sharpe's plot. There was a simple headstone with a name of the woman, her age and date of decease, and a conventional quotation from Scriptures. It was perhaps an adequate grave for a small shopkeeper's wife. Mr. Sharpe had not wanted the shame or the notoriety of a pauper's grave for his spouse.

Yet another walk back up the hill was necessary: we were at least getting healthy exercise in our jaunt!

In South Grove, which lies at the top of Swain's Lane, Holmes stood for a moment thoughtfully, then announced, "We will return to Baker Street, Watson; the matter needs to be considered over a pipe or two of tobacco!"

Back in our lodgings, I rang the bell for tea, and said, "From what I can see, Holmes, if your theory is correct, Mr. Sharpe must have committed the perfect murder!"

Holmes sat back in his favourite chair and began to pack tobacco into his pipe. "It is certainly puzzling," he admitted mildly, "but not perhaps beyond solution."

We sat in silence for an hour, Holmes ignoring his tea, although I took a strong cup to refresh myself from the day's labours. At the end of an hour or so, my friend remarked, "Well, Watson, I can think of three ways in might the matter might be accomplished. We can test at least one of them tomorrow if you care to accompany back to the scene."

The next morning I expected an early start to Highgate. I was however disappointed. "No, Watson, we will leave the matter now till well after lunch," said my friend. "Some of the investigations I need to do would be better for not being carried out in the full light of day. Fortunately, it is late enough in the year that twilight will not be long delayed."

That afternoon we took a hansom back to South Grove. Holmes indicated a building close by. "The Highgate Literary and Scientific Institution," he announced. "A worthy body. I had the honour of lecturing to the society on my methods last year, and I am sure they will allow me to use their library."

In fact on meeting us the secretary was almost embarrassingly eager to assist Sherlock Holmes. "Of course, Mr. Holmes, the resources of our society are always open to someone such as yourself," he said effusively. "Please come this way." He led us to the library at the rear of the building, which was of a fair size given that it dealt almost solely with the local matters that are the provenance of the society. "May I ask if you are currently working on a case?"

"I am indeed, sir," said Holmes, "although I am not at the moment at liberty to talk of it freely. Just at present, I would like to look at the obituary notices."

"Dear me!" said the secretary, "a murder case then?" He seemed quite excited at the idea.

"It may be, or it may not be, you understand," murmured Holmes, "at present I am simply engaged in a little research."

"Of course, of course. I quite understand. If you would come this way, we have all the back numbers of the *Times* for as far back as you could wish." He led us to a bookcase containing rows of handsomely bound copies of the *Times*. Holmes selected the latest volume and began to look for the page he needed. The secretary hovered around, clearly hoping for more information. Instead of asking for privacy, my friend engaged him in casual conversation.

"I do not suppose you have many readers that require to consult the obituary pages?" he said, turning the pages.

"In fact, Mr. Holmes, there is a surprising number. Many of our members are keen historians and need to look up dates of birth, marriage and death. For the middle and upper classes the *Times* is much more convenient than parish records."

"I see," said Holmes. "The more recent volumes then, would not be in much demand for that purpose."

"They are not as heavily used, it is true," conceded the secretary, "but we do have at least one member that owns a pawnbroker's shop and who comes in regularly to read the *Times* and look at the obituary notices. If he sees a person who lived in the neighbourhood who might have owned curiosities he takes care to call on the relatives to make an offer. He knows his business."

"Indeed," said Holmes, nodding casually. I was a little shaken by this revelation, but took care to keep my face rigid. We were close on the footsteps of Sharpe!

Finally, the secretary left us. Looking over Holmes' shoulder I saw that he was perusing the death notices for the month of Mrs. Sharpe's death. I was still puzzled by the purpose behind his search. "But Holmes," I murmured quietly so that we would not be overheard, "we know the date of Mrs. Sharpe's death, and in any case a tradesman's wife would hardly appear in the *Times*."

"True Watson: in a sense I am looking for someone like her." He continued his researches. "– Ah! Here we have something," he exclaimed.

I looked over his shoulder. It was a conventional death notice for a lady of the locality. Lady Jane Lee, a niece of the Earl of Lauderdale whose town house is on Highgate Hill. She had died at the age of forty-two. The cause of death was not given.

"How can this lady possibly be connected with our case?" I asked, confused, studying the notice. "She predeceased Mrs. Sharpe by some days."

"She may not be, indeed, but I believe there is a fair chance there is a link. Come Watson, back to the cemetery: we visit the dead!"

Back in Highgate cemetery the evening was growing dark. We found the spacious tomb of the Lauderdale family without trouble as it was near the entrance. It was constructed in the gothic fashion with a peaked roof and Grecian columns. The entrance was barred by a door of bronze, now tarnished green. Holmes inspected the lock closely with his magnifying glass. At last he straightened with an expression of satisfaction.

"Scratches, my dear Watson, around the lock: exactly what I expected to find."

"The tomb has been violated!"

"Exactly. The body of Lady Jane has been removed and was substituted for that of Mrs. Sharpe. They were about the same age, so it was only necessary that a doctor who did not know Mrs. Sharpe attended the corpse. Her family is in Derbyshire and would not expect to be able to view the body, even if the requirements of the coroner had made it possible. It was well thought out, Watson."

"But what of the real Mrs. Sharpe?"

"I am of the opinion we will find her in Lady Jane's coffin. Highgate is no longer rural enough that something as large as a corpse could escape detection for any length of time, and if he had tried the obvious course of digging in his back garden his neighbours would certainly have noticed. The empty coffin was the obvious place to secrete the body.

"It cannot even have been a crime of passion. Sharpe decided in cold blood to murder his wife, and merely waited until his doctor began his holiday to search for a woman of approximately the right age who died of some natural cause. In such a populous area as this he could be reasonably confident of finding a suitable candidate within the few weeks allowed. He then allowed some days to elapse before calling in Dr. Fletcher, using the excuse of his being away on business, so that it would be difficult to deduce the time of death."

'THE TOMB HAS BEEN VIOLATED!'

We left the cemetery. I thought to see someone standing under a willow not far away, but when I pulled at Holmes' sleeve to draw his attention to it, there was nobody there. Perhaps I had been misled by a shadow in the gloom, or possibly it was a mourner come to visit the grave of a loved one.

Turning to our right and then right again through a narrow gate, we came into the adjoining Waterlow Park. Across the park on Highgate Hill loomed the bulk of the Roman church erected there in recent years.

Inside the park, which is extensive but was quite deserted, Holmes cast up and down the picket fence that separated it from the graveyard. At last he gave an exclamation of satisfaction. "Here Watson, but be careful not to step too close: you will disturb the evidence."

Looking where he indicated, I saw two parallel tracks in the mud.

"The handcart!" I exclaimed.

"Precisely. And note that at all points the tracks are deeply marked. The cart both came and left heavily loaded. An indication that he has indeed brought his late wife to the tomb."

We walked deeper into the foliage through which that portion of the fence ran. There was a confused mass of footprints and Holmes waved me back so that he could inspect the evidence.

"Yes, it is quite clear. The handcart stood here for some little time. The footprints become much deeper as he struggles with his load. A fine task for such a lightly-built man."

Doctor as I am, and moreover hardened by the horrors of war, I shuddered at the thought of that ghastly exercise. The lifting of the wife he had murdered from the cart to his shoulders; the struggle to the tomb; the fumbling in the darkness as he substituted one body for another.

Holmes took a tape from his pocket and measured the distance between the wheel tracks, then made some measurements of the footprints, all of which he noted in his pocketbook. Finally he straightened himself. "One last step, I think Watson, before we formally give evidence against Mr. Sharpe. We will inspect his handcart, to be found if Miss Franklin is correct, in one of the farrier's stables. There will almost certainly be some traces of blood to be found and perhaps some threads of clothing."

We walked once more up the steep hill. An enquiry of an urchin gave us the position of the stable.

A thought struck me at that point. "Holmes, if you will forgive me leaving you for a few minutes I would like to take a message to Miss Franklin to set her mind at rest. Giving no details, of course, but merely saying that we have found a circumstance that will make it impossible for him to marry her."

Holmes gave a tolerant smile. "The ladies are of course your department, Watson. Do as you please. If you would have the goodness to meet me at Townsend Yard in half an hour, we will take a cab back to Baker Street."

I turned and left him, and walked briskly towards West Hill. As I passed the headquarters of the Literary and Scientific Institution I chanced to meet again with the secretary who was just leaving the building. "Dr. Watson!" he said, bowing cordially, "I trust your investigations have borne fruit?"

"Indeed," I replied, "we have only the last link to put in place."

"I am pleased to hear it. There is already much excitement at your visit. Several of the members have tried to pump me for all I know, which is, alas, almost nothing. For instance the gentleman I mentioned to you happened to come in some time later, after he had closed his shop, to read the obituaries as is his wont. He saw that the old volumes were out of their place and inquired about the circumstance. When I mentioned that they had been the objects of interest of the famous Mr. Sherlock Holmes he was much struck by the event and asked after your movements. I could tell him

181

only that you had gone on to the cemetery to continue your researches."

I started at this. Of course we had been followed! Fool that I was not to have noticed! Rudely ignoring the secretary I dashed in the direction Holmes had taken. I enquired desperately of a passer-by the location of Townsend Yard and was given directions a short way down Highgate Hill. Turning the corner I saw the open door of the stable. Behind the door, fortunately with his back to me, stood Sharpe. In his hand he held a pistol in the style of the last century; perhaps a duelling pistol from his own stock. He was peering intently into the gap between the hinged side of the door and the jamb.

I cursed the fact that I had left my service revolver at home. I did not think I would be needing it on this case. But I had brought a stout stick that day to help me up the steep slopes of the village. I moved forward, as swiftly and quietly as I could. As I did so, the villain levelled his own weapon, readying it to shoot through the gap. I gave a shout and he half turned, doubtful as to which target to aim at first. Taking advantage of his hesitation I swung my stick at his wrist. It met with a sharp crack. Sharpe dropped the pistol immediately with a shriek of agony.

I rushed at Sharpe and caught at him, but he broke away and ran pell-mell out of the yard and down the hill. Holmes darted out of the stable and took in the situation at a glance. "After him, Watson! He must not escape!" he shouted.

We followed at best speed. Highgate Hill is one of the steepest in London and the pace was hard. Sharpe was not as fast as Holmes, who with his long legs and wiry build could have won honours on the track, but he had the advantage of knowing his territory. By dodging from point to point, crossing and re-crossing the tramline that runs along the centre of the road, and leaping a fence at one point, he contrived to stay a little ahead. My sedentary habits showed themselves in my being a poor third. Halfway down the hill we came opposite the Roman church. Sharpe must have realised that he was bound to lose in a direct dash and dodged up the road to the left. We followed and soon saw his direction: he was making for the archway high above the Great North Road.

At that time the original brick and stone viaduct was in the process of being demolished to make way for the triumph of modern engineering that we know today. Directly over the old structure the engineers had so far placed seven huge cast-iron arcs as the support for the new roadway. Sharpe clambered down on to the old arch, darting between the mounds of rubble and rubbish that lay about. In the darkness and with places of concealment I feared he stood a real chance of evading us or of doubling back.

"Keep after him, Watson!" shouted my friend. He himself turned and ran towards the new bridge. With my heart in my mouth I watched him run up on to the nearest of the great cast-iron beams. The beam was over a foot wide, and would not have been considered difficult had it been a short distance from the ground, but as it was it needed ice-cool nerves to ignore the dreadful drop to the great highway below us.

I realised it was Holmes' intention to cut off the miscreant and followed Sharpe, driving him perforce on to the shattered remains of the old structure. He clambered frantically over the stonework, widening the gap between us with his natural agility. Then glancing ahead he caught sight of Holmes who had now reached the other side and was moving towards him. He stopped and looked desperately in every direction. Holmes and I closed on him, confident now of capture. In this we were mistaken: Sharpe still had one way of escape and took it. With a despairing shriek he leapt over the remains of the parapet and plunged fifty feet to the roadway below.

Shouts came up from below. Holmes joined me and plucked at my sleeve. "Come, Watson, we can do no good here. Sharpe has at least been spared the gallows which would otherwise undoubtedly have been his fate."

The final step had to be done through the proper channels. Holmes sent a message to Scotland Yard outlining his suspicions and a certificate of exhumation was quickly procured through the local magistrate. A gloomy gathering ensued a few days later in Highgate cemetery outside the Lauderdale tomb. The curator of the cemetery was present, as well as Inspector Lestrade and one of his constables; Dr. Hugh Smith, Mrs. Sharpe's physician; a very elegant gentleman named Gallienne who represented the interests of the Lauderdale family; Holmes and myself.

The curator produced his key and we all entered, removing our hats as we did so. The tomb was crowded in an undignified manner as we grouped ourselves round the bier. The constable, a burly man, produced a screwdriver and with some labour removed the many fastenings. With the assistance of the curator, the lid of the handsome casket, still looking very new, was removed and placed to one side. Inside the coffin, the silk lining of which was splattered with blood, lay the disfigured corpse of a middle-aged woman. At her side was a long and shiny wooden object. Holmes reached in with no expression of distaste but rather of satisfaction and grasped it. "The knobkerrie!" he exclaimed. "The last link in our investigations."

Dr. Smith spoke formally: "Inspector, I can identify this person as my former patient Mrs. Dorothy Sharpe of Highgate West Hill."

Lestrade nodded to his constable, who produced his notebook and a pencil and laboriously wrote down the words. "Thank you, doctor," he said, then turning to the curator said, "We have obtained an exhumation order for the Sharpe grave as well, sir, which I will show you in your office. I must ask you to get a couple of your sextons to dig up the coffin and place it unopened in the chapel until we find someone to identify the corpse. No doubt Mr. Holmes is right and we'll find it's Lady Jane. If so, we'll apply to the coroner to re-open both the inquests."

"Re-open the inquests!" cried Mr. Gallienne in horror. "Gentlemen: I must insist that nothing is done in haste. This whole matter will be most embarrassing to his lordship. The fact that his relative's body should have been treated in this cavalier fashion will be intensely distasteful to one of his refined sensibilities. I must beg of you that the matter be treated with the utmost discretion."

He pulled himself together with an effort. "Inspector: the Home Secretary, Sir Spencer Walpole, or a senior member of his staff will be in touch with you early tomorrow morning regarding the handling of this case. You will have the goodness to take no further action until you hear from him. Mr. Holmes, I suppose I must congratulate you on your perspicacity, although on my word it might have been better to let the thing be. His lordship will wish to pay your fees in full and at a generous rate. It is however vital that no breath of this scandal leaks out."

Holmes bowed in his saturnine fashion. "Sir, I live for my work. I have no taste for the notoriety that Watson has brought me and for my part I willingly accede to your request. It is perhaps fortunate for you that Sharpe is dead, as no man can be denied a trial."

Lestrade looked mutinous at this interference with his duties, but Gallienne had his way, and I saw no hint of the story in the papers. No doubt the inquests were held *in camera* and the papers deposited on the confidential shelves at Kew. So it is that I leave this story, one of the most macabre of all Holmes' exploits, to a future time.

THE MYSTERY OF THE MISSING RUBIES

NE morning late in the year 1893, Holmes and I were seated at breakfast. It was unusually cold that winter, and from the broad window of our sitting room I could see that an overnight sprinkling of snow on Baker Street had already been turned to black slush by the feet of passers-by and the wheels of the vehicles. The sky was overcast; the air clammy and the whole scene had a depressing effect on me. Mrs. Hudson had brought the post, and we were both indulging in the Bohemian pleasure of reading whilst we ate.

"Here is an interesting note, Watson," said my friend. "It is from some cousins of mine in Yorkshire. They are inviting both myself and my brother Mycroft to spend Christmas with them in their house in the West Riding. They no doubt feel sorry for a couple of old bachelors!"

"And will you accept?"

"Upon my word, I think I will! Much as I love London, she is not at her best at this time of year. A short holiday in the country will do me good, and I will return refreshed in the New Year."

I took care not to show my feelings of course, but my heart sank. I had no family that I felt I could impose on at this season, and with Holmes away, my Christmas would perforce be a lonely one.

"You will accompany me I trust, Watson?" asked Holmes.

"I? But Holmes, I am no member of your family; I could not possibly intrude on your cousins."

"Nonsense! In Yorkshire they see so few new faces that a visitor is always most welcome. They will sit entranced for hours by your stories of life in the bustling metropolis. There will certainly be room, as they have a large house, and apart from the servants there is only their little boy living with them."

"Well, it would certainly be delightful to spend Christmas in the country. Perhaps if you approached them very delicately, so as to give them every chance to refuse, I could agree."

"I will telegraph to them when we have finished our meal. The telegram is, alas, rather a blunt instrument. It does not lend itself to delicacy of touch, but I will do my best!"

So it was that a few days before Christmas, Holmes and I took a train from St. Pancras. A speedy and comfortable trip brought us in a few hours to the village of Clapham, in the Yorkshire Dales. Outside the little station, a brougham was waiting for us. The driver, a cheerful, red-faced character, introduced himself as Postlethwaite. Whipping up the horses, we set out at a brisk trot. At those northerly latitudes, the weather was of course much colder than in London, and a thick blanket of snow lay all about. I gazed about me appreciatively. The view was of a lattice of hillside fields, each bordered by carefully-built drystone walls; behind them on the higher slopes were sheer cliffs and an occasional clump of trees; they all combined to soothe the soul of one who has spent too much time in the endless streets of our great capital.

After about an hour, the road began to climb steadily upward. Above us we saw a looming mountain, on one side it showed a precipitous slope to its highest point, and on the other a more gradual descent towards the west. With its dark colouring it looked like a great beast lying watchfully across the land.

"What is that mountain, Postlethwaite?" I inquired.

"That's Pen-y-ghent, sir, one of the Three Peaks. You'll see it well from the house."

It was not long before we turned off the road through a pair of stone gateposts and up the drive to the house. It was a sizeable affair, built about fifty years previously by one of the great wool barons as his country dwelling. It was constructed, as are even humble cottages in this area, of large limestone blocks, having a mainly dark yellow tint.

The family came to the door to greet us. Holmes' cousin, a tall and strongly-built man named John Parsons, wrung his hand in welcome.

"Welcome to Yorkshire, Doctor Watson!" he said to me with the utmost good will as he took my hand in turn.

I was then introduced to his wife, a young and charming woman, and to their son, Christopher, a stout little lad about three years of age. Despite his youth, he did not cling to his mother's skirts, but came boldly forward to inspect us, and solemnly tolerated our shaking his hand.

Holmes and I gave up our coats and sticks and all proceeded to the large drawing room, to take a very welcome cup of coffee. There we were introduced to Roderick Keighley, Mrs. Parson's brother, who was also spending Christmas at the house. He rose to take our hands and murmured some appropriate words. I noted that he had little in common with his sister, being a dark and saturnine man, where she was fair and of a cheerful disposition.

"Have you heard from Mycroft?" asked Holmes.

"We had a telegram from him this morning," said John. "He expects to be with us before lunch tomorrow."

"Excellent! He will be able to come for a brisk walk with us tomorrow afternoon."

There was general laughter at this: Mycroft was renowned for both his laziness and his girth.

We were taken to adjoining rooms, and as Postlethwaite had predicted, I had a superb view of Pen-y-ghent from the window. Whether accompanied by Mycroft or not, I looked forward to an invigorating walk along the snowy lanes.

The dinner that evening was plain country cooking, but good and ample. Christopher was considered by his indulgent parents old enough to sit with us, and perched in a high chair next to his mother. Also at table was his nurse, Miss Beck, a very pretty girl of about twenty years of age. She came from Ilkley, but had very little of the local accent. I must confess that her sharply-defined features and high colouring made a favourable impression on me.

Mrs. Parsons wore a long coffee-coloured gown, trimmed with lace, and about her neck wore a magnificent jewelled necklace. The stones appeared to be rubies, but they had been cut in the style more usually associated with emeralds; that is, oblong and chamfered at the edges. The gold setting was light and delicate and the whole effect was most elegant. I complimented her on her appearance.

"You are too kind, Dr. Watson," she replied. "You may think it too grand for a family dinner, but we get so few chances to show our finery out here. Occasionally we attend balls in Leeds or Lancaster, but both are so distant that it is a rare treat. And so I indulge myself whenever we have guests."

"The gay life is naturally important to a young person like yourself, but for my part I would be content with the life of the Dales. I feel so comfortable and relaxed here already that I dread returning to the scrimmage of London. I would set myself up in practice in these parts if it were not for the fact that as everybody is so confoundedly healthy, I should be sure of starving to death!"

Everybody laughed, but Holmes put in lightly, "There is always the worthy Postlewaithe. His elbow still pains him from when he fell from his charger years ago."

Mrs. Parsons looked surprised, "He has told you of his cavalry days already? You must have made a remarkable impression on him: he is usually as taciturn as any good Yorkshireman."

"He told me nothing, but I saw at once from his bearing and address that he was an old soldier, and from the way he handled the horse on the drive here I saw that he had a natural affinity for the animal, and also that he had at some fairly distant time broken his left elbow. Damage to the elbow is of course a very typical injury resulting from a fall from a horse."

"Remarkable! You are quite right: he served in the Fifth Lancers in India under my father, Colonel Keighley. When his injuries prevented him serving any longer, my father took him into his household, and from there he has come into ours."

"Your father shows a very commendable concern for his soldiers," I said.

Mrs. Parsons sighed. "Indeed, but there are so many that need help. I fear that in this area alone there are dozens who have been so terribly wounded in the service of their Queen and country that they are no longer able to earn a living, and so they live constantly on the edge of starvation, and meet at last an early end from pain and deprivation. I constantly ask John to do more for them."

John Parsons looked at little annoyed at this. "You have indeed mentioned it many times my dear," he said, "and I have as often given it as my opinion that most of them are idle rogues who could perfectly well work if they cared to, and if they were not always being given money by folk whose hearts too often rule their heads."

Mrs. Parson's lips tightened. "You are unfair, John. The wars we engage in constantly to bring enlightenment and true religion to the less fortunate of this world take a terrible toll of our young men. It is our duty to care for them. If the Queen's cousin, the Marquis of Granby, sets such an example, can we do less?"

"He is another who is too ready to listen to a glib story. I declare that if he gives much more of his fortune away, every public house in England will be named after him!"

It was clear that a family quarrel was developing, so I turned the subject hastily. "I was hoping to do some shooting while I am here. Is it good country for that?"

"It is," said John Parsons politely. "The moors are full of grouse and hares, and as there are few trees, you will often get very sporting shots at extreme range. Roderick here is an excellent shot, perhaps you could take Dr. Watson with you when you next go out, Roderick?"

"Certainly," said Roderick indifferently, not raising his eyes from his plate.

"And you must borrow one of my weapons," went on John, ignoring his brother-in-law's offhand manner. "I believe you will find an acceptable selection in the gunroom. I will take you there tomorrow."

"You are more than kind."

The next morning showed a leaden sky, heavy with the promise of snow. Postlethwaite set off early for Clapham to meet Mycroft. Soon after he left the first flakes began to fall, gently at first, but then faster and faster till we began to worry as to whether the train would get through.

I read a novel for a hour or two, but finding it unrewarding decided to go in search of human companionship. Looking in at the schoolroom, I found Miss Beck with her charge, who was playing with a large toy fort.

"Bang! Bang!" he exclaimed as I entered.

I smiled at the little man. "I'm a friend," I protested, "a true British soldier like yourself."

Christopher looked at me doubtfully, "Where's your red coat if you're a soldier? All soldiers wear red coats. I want a red coat."

"Well, I've got one at home," I said, "but actually I've left the army now. I was wounded, you see."

Christopher brightened up at this. "Did they shoot you?"

"Indeed they did. Through the shoulder. Very painful it was too."

Miss Beck looked concerned. "I'm so sorry, Dr. Watson, I hope you are quite recovered now?"

"I still get a twinge or two in damp weather, but it is nothing really. Many of my comrades never left Afghanistan, so I count myself tolerably fortunate.

"Now, young man, shall we have a look at your strategy?" I bent over the fort, which was stoutly made of wood panelling. Slit windows had been cut with a fretsaw and a pair of gates with a working bolt let into the front. It was complete with ramparts along which lead soldiers in various postures were patrolling or threatening with their weapons.

"Do you know who these are?" I asked, pointing to men with blue shakoes and sashes.

"They're the sappers. They dig trenches and things."

Miss Beck laughed. "He knows all the regimentals. Postlethwaite often plays with him and has taught him all about the army. He made the fort, as well."

"Capital! Well, your men are well set out; you have them guarding the gate from both sides: that's always a weak point. And you have men at the corners: that's good too; they can command two sides of the fort at once. Just one matter you're weak on, General: and that is you have no men at the windows. You need them there if the enemy get too close and shelter under the walls so you can't get at them from the battlements."

Christopher's face looked glum. "I haven't got enough soldiers. I can only put them on the walls."

"Christmas is coming, my dear," said Miss Beck archly. "Perhaps some more little soldiers will come marching up to enlist."

The boy did not look entirely convinced by this, but was mollified enough to ignore us both and continue with his battle. Miss Beck and I sat at one of the windows and passed the time in amiable chatter.

The schoolroom windows faced the front of the house, so I was able to observe with relief the trap returning. Postlethwaite was at the reins, but I would not have recognised him, covered as he was with snow, and his head sunk deeply in his muffler.

We both hurried down to the door, and were in time to greet Mycroft as he hurried his bulk into the house. I noticed that his boots and the trousers below the knee were sodden. Postlethwaite followed on his heels with Mycroft's bags, dumped them unceremoniously in a corner, then left to stable the horse. All sighed in relief as the door closed on the wind and swirling snow.

"Ha! Ha!" said Mycroft, "It's good to be indoors again, but I fear it will be some time before we Londoners can return to our usual haunts."

"We are snowed in, you mean?" asked John Parsons.

"There is no question of it. I had to get out and push on that last confounded hill, or I'd be out there yet!"

"There is no cause for concern," put in Mrs. Parsons. "We are cut off about one year in three, so we are quite used to it and have ample supplies of food and fuel. The only danger might be boredom, but with such good company there is little fear of that!"

Mycroft was taken to his room at once to change, and soon after joined us in front of a blazing fire in the sitting room. It was only mid-afternoon, but so bad was the weather that the lamps had to be lit. The maid brought in tea, and we all fell to, Mycroft putting away vast quantities of cakes and biscuits, then entertaining us hugely with a succession of stories. He was a great clubman, and seemed to know all the most eminent people, and to have an anecdote about each one of them.

"The Prime Minister, now," he roared, "was in White's one evening last week, eating his dinner with a good appetite. He told me later that he had had no breakfast because he was closeted with his Secretary who was giving him the latest details on the Crimean situation, and he had had no lunch because the Queen had unexpectedly commanded his presence in order that she too could hear the latest news, and no tea because he had to take part in a major debate on Crimea. Finally he was able to leave, came to the club and ordered his favourite meal: lamb chops with boiled potatoes and green beans. Just as the waiter put it in front of him, a messenger came from his wife reminding him that they were due at a reception for the French Ambassador, which he had completely forgotten. Without hesitation, he grabbed his cutlery, and began cramming large chunks of meat and entire potatoes into his mouth at the fastest speed he could manage. He finished the entire plate in under two minutes, rose and ran from the dining room!"

We all laughed immoderately at the vision of the impeccable Mr. Gladstone, whose careful and moderate eating habits were held up as an example to every young child in the land, eating his dinner in such a fashion.

We passed some time in this pleasant fashion, then dispersed to go about our various interests; I to the library to sort through some business papers and write a few letters. It was ironic, I felt, that now I had the leisure to catch up on my correspondence, I was unable to post it.

At seven o'clock, I gathered all together, preparatory to my going to my room to prepare for dinner. I had just reached the entrance hall, when there came a sharp cry from above. I heard swift steps being taken, and then Mrs. Parsons leant over the balustrade at the first floor.

"Dr. Watson, will you please find my husband at once and ask him to come to our room? The most dreadful thing has happened!"

I ran immediately to the study, where I found John Parsons and Sherlock Holmes in conversation, and delivered my message. All three of us then hurried upstairs, where we found Mrs. Parsons dressed in one of her fine gowns but looking distraught. In one corner, her maid, Brooke, was in tears.

"My rubies, John: they've disappeared!" she exclaimed to her husband. His face at once took on a grim aspect.

"I see," he said, "and when did you last see them?"

"I put them in my jewel box last night, as always. I had no occasion to look in the box during the day, then just now I opened it to take out the necklace and it was missing. I called Brooke at once, thinking that perhaps she had taken them to be polished, but she had not."

Sherlock Holmes put in a question. "Apart from you, your husband and your maid, does anyone else have access to your room?"

"No-one at all. Brooke does such cleaning as is required and lights the fire and brings me my morning tea."

"Then I think we must assume theft."

"That is impossible," said John Parsons hotly. "My servants are beyond reproach: most of them have been with me since my own childhood. And as for my guests, they are all, apart from yourself of course doctor, my close relations."

"It is certainly a problem. But I beg you not to distress yourself: the rubies can at least not leave this house while the snow lies so deep, and in the meantime I have every hope of finding the person responsible."

Dinner that evening was a gloomy affair. Mrs. Parsons was sunk in misery, and ate little and spoke less. Mr. Parsons was in a furious mood, and sat with a brow as black as thunder, also speaking to no one. In the circumstances, none of the rest of us felt able to make any remarks beyond those of necessity.

After dinner, Sherlock took himself off to Mrs. Parson's room with his magnifying glass. An hour or so later, he joined Mycroft and myself in the library to discuss his findings.

"The room shows nothing beyond the usual marks of occupancy. I believe the thief merely took his chance and walked in. As the room is at the head of the stairs, we must all pass it to go to our own bedrooms, and I am sure that you have observed that the door is often left open. The dressing table is on the far wall: the culprit could have taken three strides, purloined the rubies, and escaped in less time than it takes to tell.

"I find on enquiry that the servants have their bedrooms at the back of the house, reached by a separate stair. They would none of them, apart from Brooke in the course of her duties, have ordinary occasion to go up the main flight. The exception is Miss Beck, whose room is next to the boy's."

Mycroft grunted. "So those with the opportunity would be Brooke, Miss Beck, Roderick Keighley, ourselves – and of course Mr. and Mrs. Parsons."

"They would hardly steal from themselves!" I laughed.

Sherlock raised a quizzical eyebrow, while Mycroft gave a sharp snort of derision.

"On the contrary, my dear Watson," said my friend, "Mrs. Parsons is a prime suspect. Consider: she has a generous nature and would like to help those she knows to be in distress through no fault of their own. But her husband has amongst his other virtues those typically Yorkshire ones of thrift and scepticism and will give her nothing. Is it not possible that she has secreted them and at the first opportunity will sell them in order to use the money for a cause she considers so worthy?"

"Well, it might be possible – but surely, you saw her distress at the dinner table not two hours ago!"

"My gallant Watson! Nothing brings out the parfait gentle knight in you like a woman's tears! Let us leave Mrs. Parsons aside for the moment then, and consider the other possibilities."

"Roderick Keighley, of course."

"Certainly he is a suspect. He is the youngest of Colonel Keighley's three sons, and so will have few prospects. He might well persuade himself that it is no more than her sisterly duty to help him when he is in need of cash, and by helping himself he does no more than avoid an embarrassing scene with her husband."

"He is surely the guilty party," I said. "Brooke has been Mrs. Parson's maid for many years, and it is obvious that Miss Beck has nothing of the criminal in her."

Holmes smiled, "Brooke I might pass, but Miss Beck I cannot. She is clearly from a family of some quality: so much we can tell from her speech and her manner. And yet she has taken a lowly, if honourable, post as a nurse. We must draw the conclusions that either she is estranged from her family, or that they have fallen on hard times and she must take what work she can. A young woman might become resentful and feel that it is not just that her employer has so much while she has so little, and seek to redress the balance."

"I cannot believe it!"

Holmes shrugged. "The possibilities exist; I say no more. Many hypotheses may be built, but without data it is not clear which, if any, is the true one."

"That's the trouble," grunted Mycroft, "Data. All we know is that the rubies were swiped. Now we must watch the others. They must not be allowed to leave the house. There are a thousand places where the jewels might be hidden on these confounded moors, then retrieved perhaps months later when the hue and cry has died down."

"We can hardly keep them here against their will," I ventured.

"A few days only," said Mycroft, "then between myself and my young brother, we will without question have got to the bottom of this affair."

"Perhaps it will not be a problem, then. With the snow lying at least two feet deep outside, and drifting up to six, anyone would need a very ingenious explanation for a walk."

The next day I was proved wrong. It was only an hour after breakfast that glancing back I observed Roderick, enveloped in a greatcoat and carrying a gun and a game bag, making for the door.

"Hi!" I said quickly. "Where are you off to?"

"Where does it look like?" said he, ungraciously, although of course my tone had inadvertently been sharp. "I'm going to do a little shooting. I'll be back before tea."

"Oh, but I should like to come with you," I said quickly.

"Some other time, perhaps."

Very fortunately, John Parsons appeared at that moment, and took my part. "Come, come, Roderick," he protested, "you promised Dr. Watson only the night before last that you would take him out and show him some sport. Please wait just a few minutes while we equip him."

"Oh, very well," said Roderick ungraciously. He was obviously most reluctant to take me, but even more reluctant

198

to offend his rich brother-in-law. I strove to keep an impartial viewpoint: his attitude might arise merely from the fact that he preferred his own company. All the same, I vowed to watch him like a hawk.

John Parsons took me to the gunroom. It was small, but well equipped, including with a workbench on which I saw tools and fluids for the stripping and cleaning of the weapons. Several modern rifles were present, mostly Lee Enfields. There was an enormous elephant gun, fully 0.5 calibre from the look of it, which hung on the wall. Some pistols, including two matched pairs of antique duelling pistols lay under a glass case. The bulk of the collection was made up of shotguns; there were at least twenty pair present.

I commented on the number and John explained: "I am in the habit of inviting parties of my friends to join me in August for some grouse shooting on the moors hereabout. There is nothing like it for good exercise, good fellowship and good sport."

"You are very hospitable."

"I do it for my own pleasure as much as anything. Now, let us see. This Purdey here seems about your reach; would you care to try it?"

He took down from a rack a beautifully carved example of the gunsmith's art. The stock was mahogany, and the metalwork carved with a scene of a duck starting up from the reeds as a pair of dogs gave tongue. The whole effect was wrapped around the stock, the hammer (which was represented as a bunch of opening reeds) and the trigger guard, so that it could not be seen from one point only, but rather displayed itself a piece at a time as the weapon moved.

I put it to my shoulder and sighted along it. It was beautifully balanced. "A very fine gun, I must declare!" I said, "I don't believe I've ever handled a better."

"A shotgun can never really be part of you unless it has been made to order, I am afraid. But you should get some good sport, nevertheless. Now, let me give you some cartridges. These filled with no. 15 shot will do for grouse, and these no. 20 for rabbit or hare. If you keep one in each barrel, you will be ready for most things."

Waving away my earnest thanks, he led the way out of the gunroom and carefully locked the door. "I wish you good shooting, Doctor. My only regret is that I cannot come with you, but so near the end of the year the affairs of the estate take a great deal of my time. I hope you will give us a full description of your sport over tea this afternoon."

I took my leave of him and hurried to my room to dress for a day outdoors. I was as quick as could be managed, but nevertheless found Roderick visibly chafing at the delay.

"Come on then," he said shortly, and without another word led the way into the snow.

We walked to the back of the house, and then clambered up a stiff slope. It was not easy, especially given that we did not wish to place our guns on the snow. Fortunately, many pieces of limestone stood proud of the turf, and by using these as handholds or footholds as the occasion presented itself, we made quite good progress. At the end of a strenuous half-hour, we found ourselves on a broadly horizontal, but hillocked expanse. It formed as it were, a broad step in the ascent to Pen-y-ghent, which now towered close above us.

"What is this called?" I asked.

"This is Blea Fell," replied my companion, "but we're going over to Newby Moss, just there: the game prefer it."

The walking was easier now, but the distance was almost two miles. As we walked I attempted conversation.

"Do you often get the chance to shoot?"

"As often as I can, but not as often as I'd like."

"It is certainly very useful having a sister with a big house in the Dales."

"My sister has nothing of the kind: it's my brother-in-law that has a big house in the Dales."

"That is what I meant, of course."

A grunt was the only reply, and I saved my breath for walking.

A few yards further, and a hare started up almost at our feet. It raced in a curving line for a pile of boulders, its legs pumping furiously and its ears held tight to the skull. We both raised our guns to our shoulders, though Roderick was quicker, and fired; our shots making a double bang. The hare leaped, somersaulted, and lay dead. With a chuckle of satisfaction, Roderick strolled over, picked up the carcass and pushed it into his game bag.

"Which of us hit it?" I ventured.

"I did."

We came shortly to Newby Moss, which was flat enough to be farmed, and was divided up into fields by the characteristic drystone walls. We climbed the first, and then Roderick suggested, "Shall we form a line? It's better that way: you get up twice as much game, and with any luck we can both get a shot at most of it."

I strongly suspected that he merely wished not to have to make conversation with me, but I assented: I could still watch his movements. We separated by about forty feet, and walked slowly down the field. We had found nothing by the time we came to the far boundary, and both began to climb over the wall at convenient points. It was not easy, because the walls are at chest height, and the topmost stones rocked alarmingly. At last I was perched standing on top and about to jump down on to the turf on the far side, when I heard a terrific bang, and was thrown violently backwards into the field I had just left.

As I lay there dazed, I became aware of a pain in my left forearm. I heard Roderick running up, and feared for my life: was he coming to finish me off? I groped about me for my shotgun, but it had been flung far away. I could see blood on the snow. I rolled myself to face him, hoping at least to get some warning, but he flung his gun down and bent over me with every appearance of concern.

'I HEARD A TERRIFIC BANG, AND WAS THROWN
VIOLENTLY BACKWARDS'

"Are you alright? Where did I hit you?"

"In the arm." I attempted to raise it, but desisted at once.

Roderick produced a stout knife from his gamebag and slit the sleeve from the wrist. Turning the sleeve back he inspected the wound.

"Not too bad, I think. There's a lot of blood, and a lot of punctures, but nothing big enough to do real damage. Now, can you walk, do shall I run for help?"

"Help me sit up."

He did so, and I sat a while, recovering myself. At last, I heaved myself to my feet, Roderick helping me.

"I think I can do it."

"Good man. Put your right arm round my shoulder, and we'll get started."

We went slowly, and twice Roderick had to leave me standing while he kicked a gap out of a drystone wall. However, our way led mostly downhill and as we went on the wound became more numb. At last we came in sight of the house. Roderick shouted and Postlethwaite and one of the grooms came out to help. I was carried into the sitting room and laid tenderly on a couch.

"Watson! What has happened to you?" said Sherlock Holmes as he strode to my side.

"I've been shot in the arm. Nothing too serious: there is no need for concern."

"Indeed," said my friend, giving Roderick a murderous glance, "that is fortunate, as there is no chance of getting a doctor here and we must tend you ourselves. May I ask what happened?"

"My fault," explained Roderick, "I was getting up on a wall, when I caught the trigger in one of the buttons on my coat. Damn' silly really, I shouldn't have left it cocked, but we hadn't seen much sport and I didn't want to lose a chance."

Miss Beck hurried into the room. "My poor Dr. Watson! Is there anything I can do? I nursed my dear father in his last years, so I have some experience of sickbeds."

203

"There is certainly something you can do, if the sight of blood is not distasteful to you," I said as heartily as I could. "If you could get a bowl of hot water, a pair of tweezers, some towels and some clean linen for bandages, I shall instruct you in the procedure."

"I shall bring them at once."

She hurried off. Holmes talked to me generally about the conditions on the moors, but was obviously constrained in Roderick's presence. On Miss Beck's return, he took his leave. "We will leave you with your patient, but will not be far away. Please call if there is anything you need."

They both left. Miss Beck placed the bowl on the rug and knelt by the couch. With a pair of scissors, she cut away the coat and shirtsleeves at the elbow, then tenderly wiped away the blood. I peered at the damage. There was a broad band of punctures in the fleshy part of the forearm, but on the opposite side from the radial artery. I sighed: it could have been much worse, but after Afghanistan I felt I had had my turn of being a target.

"What you must do, my dear Miss Beck, is to pick out the shot piece by piece with your tweezers. There is one ball in each puncture: you must go as deep as is necessary."

Without further prompting, she began work. Some were shallow, and some devilishly deep. I grit my teeth and tried not to groan. As for the lady, she searched my face anxiously when she had to probe deeply, and after a few minutes began to cry silently at her work. At last she was done. At my instructions, she rolled the linen, wound it tightly round the arm and fastened it by ripping the ends and knotting them back.

"There, it is done."

Instinctively, I reached out with my good arm and embraced her. In the emotion of the moment she responded and moved into my embrace. We kissed passionately and at length. Her young, strong body pressed against mine, and for a time we were conscious of nothing save each other.

After a little time, however, she recollected herself and gently released herself from my arms. Rising to her feet, she smiled at me, smoothing her hair as she did so in a woman's instinctive gesture.

"You are free with your nurses, Dr. Watson," she said lightly. "I am sure they must compete to work for you, if those are the wages they receive."

For my part, I saw no humour in the situation. I was weak and trembling from the effects of the wound, the hard exercise, and the storm of emotion that this raged through me. "My dear Miss Beck," I stumbled, "I can only profoundly apologise for my conduct. I had no excuse for imposing on your youth and inexperience."

Her reply was to raise one eyebrow. "If there is any fault Doctor, it was as much on my part as yours. If you wish, I will dismiss the incident from my mind."

"I do not ask you to do that."

"I will leave you now to rest; Mr. Sherlock Holmes and Mr. Mycroft Holmes will naturally be anxious to see you, shall I ask them to wait, say, one hour?"

"Thank you; I am sure I will be greatly recovered by then."

Miss Beck gathered together the equipment she had brought and left the room. I lay on the couch in a troubled state for a little time, but sleep soon overtook me.

I awoke to find Sherlock Holmes and his brother sitting in armchairs a few yards away. My friend, leaning back with his hands steepled together appeared to be in deep thought. Mycroft sat forward, his arms on his knees, also appeared to be conceptualising a problem in his own fashion.

"How good of you both to visit me!" I exclaimed, sitting myself up with a little effort.

"My dear Watson, how glad I am to see you so recovered!" said my friend. "Your sleep and the attentions of Miss Beck have obviously done wonders."

"It is not so bad," I said gingerly moving the injured arm, "I believe I will be on my feet tomorrow, although I will wear a sling for a few days."

"Your incident has at least had the advantage of giving us more data," growled Mycroft.

"Indeed?" I said. "Your suspicions of Roderick Keighley are then confirmed?"

"On the contrary," said my friend, "we are convinced it was a genuine accident. We have examined the shot that Miss Beck removed from your arm and found it to be no. 10 – that is, for birds and small game. Now he would at least have loaded no. 20 if he wished to kill, and further, a sportsman of Roderick Keighley's experience would be certain to hit you squarely and not merely wing you. No, it is on Miss Beck that our suspicions converge."

"What evidence have you found?"

"Her recent behaviour towards yourself is at the least highly questionable."

"What the devil do you mean by that, Holmes?" I said hotly, feeling the blood rising to my face.

Sherlock Holmes and Mycroft both laughed heartily. "Come, come, Watson!" said my friend jocularly. "There is no need to be modest: the ladies were ever your department. It was clear enough from Miss Beck's deportment and disarray what she had been about, even if we did not have the evidence of your own present reaction."

"Even supposing the matter was as you say," said I, "what possible bearing can it have on the theft of the rubies?"

"Only that if she is the culprit, she might think it useful to have at least one person firmly on her side from affection, or if that failed, we may always suppose, blackmail."

"I cannot believe it!"

"Perhaps. I admit that a woman's motives are not always susceptible of logical analysis. But Mycroft here has also been busy."

"I have been observing the little boy's movements," grunted Mycroft, "and I see that he is not considered to need

206

constant attention. Between the hours of ten and twelve, and again between three and five, he is given regular tuition in the schoolroom by Miss Beck. He is also supervised by Miss Beck on waking, on going to bed and at all mealtimes. There are, however, gaps in this schedule, and I have on several occasions noticed him toddling about the house unsupervised. Once he went to the kitchen for a word with the cook and perhaps a brandy ball or two. No doubt he often goes to his mother's room. Now, what could be more natural that Miss Beck should see the lad in his mother's room and escort him from it? And what could be easier to arrange deliberately? So we see that she could armour herself against all risk of being discovered by these means. Also, as a permanent inhabitant of the house, she has a thousand hiding places for the jewels, and a thousand opportunities of recovering them, perhaps in many months time. Roderick Keighley, though, is an infrequent visitor."

"You build a convincing case, certainly," I said, with a heavy heart, "but still I do not believe she is capable of such duplicity as you describe."

"We shall see," said my friend. "The matter is far from being proven as yet."

We left the problem there. A little later dinner was served, and I felt well enough to take my place at table. I found difficulty in eating with one hand, although the maid cut the meat small for me before serving. After dinner, I did not stay for the brandy and conversation, but pleading my trying day went to bed early.

The next morning dawned bright and cold. It was Christmas Eve, and after breakfast Postlethwaite went out on to the estate and came back with a well-formed pine about seven feet tall as a Christmas tree. He set it securely in a large earthenware pot in the far corner of the sitting room, and after lunch the whole family turned out to dress the tree. Mrs. Parsons did most of the work, but the rest of us assisted. The exception was Mycroft who sat his great bulk in a chair and watched us tolerantly. We draped on the tinsel, hung bright paper stars from the boughs and placed red and white candles about. Sherlock Holmes' unusual height and reach were called on to place the angel at the very top. Christopher was of course very excited. He was allowed to place some objects but his chubby little hands dislodged as much or more as they positioned.

Later, John Parsons gave orders to hang holly boughs about the room, that we might also have a more traditionally English decoration.

When the task was finished, we went about our occupations. I did not seek out Miss Beck; I felt that my position was dishonourable, and could not feel it right that a short time after enjoying her embraces I was closeted with those who suspected her of a crime. For her part, Miss Beck gave no sign that anything was other than as usual. Towards the evening she offered to change my bandage, to which I consented. We were however not alone during this operation and so I was spared most of the embarrassment I might have felt.

Perhaps because of the season, John Parsons had not mentioned the matter of the missing rubies. That evening he could contain himself no longer, and asked myself, Sherlock Holmes and Mycroft to join him in his study.

"I must ask you, gentlemen, have you any clues as to the thief of my wife's necklace? It is now three days since its disappearance and I confess that I fear that it may be gone for ever."

Sherlock Holmes took it upon himself to answer. "We have indications of a trail, and I still have every hope of resolving this matter in time. There are after all very few possibilities."

John Parsons shook his head sadly. "It is because the possibilities are few that I am most distressed. Whoever should prove to be the culprit, it will be someone very close to me that I have trusted and who has shamefully betrayed me. I would almost rather sacrifice the thousand pounds the jewels cost than endure that knowledge."

My friend bowed in sympathy. Soon after we took our leave.

Christmas morning was another glorious day. I pulled back the curtains of my room and looked at the sparkling fells climbing up to the sky and felt the joy of living. My arm was feeling much better and I thought I could risk leaving off the sling.

At breakfast we wished each other the compliments of the season. It was of course impossible to attend the church in Settle that the family usually visited, but at eleven o'clock John Parsons called the whole household together and held a short prayer service. I regret to say that the cook fidgeted the entire time, obviously fretting that her goose was not being attended to.

Presents were exchanged, and I was delighted to receive a swordstick from Sherlock Holmes. It was a fine one, with excellent balance made by James Smith and Sons of New Oxford Street. I drew the sword rather awkwardly one-handed and practised a few passes. I had no doubt that it would prove its worth in due course on one of our expeditions.

We gathered again before the fire, and Christopher was indulged to the extent of being allowed to play on the hearthrug. He had been overjoyed to receive an entire box of lead soldiers, most exquisitely painted. He lined them up in battalions and marched them about the rug, making warlike noises as he did so.

"Well, my boy, your reinforcements have arrived!" I said. "Your fort will have all the defenders it needs, and it is not every general that can say that."

"Yes," the little lad answered, "won't need those fat ones any longer."

"Fat soldiers?" I said, "Certainly you must be firm. A few more long patrols and they'll be as fit as you please."

"No. They fall over too."

Sherlock Holmes raised his head sharply at this exchange and spoke to the boy. "Who gave you your fat soldiers, Christopher?"

"Found them. In Mamma's room."

We all looked at each other in growing realisation and delight. Then the whole company, except for the child who looked bewildered, began laughing.

"Come!" said my friend, leaping to his feet, "let us go to the fort and discharge these inefficient soldiers!"

We ascended the stairs at a good pace, John Parsons catching his son up in his arms and Mycroft panting at the rear. Entering the schoolroom in a body, we all crowded round the fort while Sherlock Holmes fell to his knees and peered in through the gate. He inserted his hand into the fort, and then withdrew it, clutching the magnificent chain of rubies. Everybody cheered and cried their congratulations.

"Your necklace, madam," said Holmes with a bow as he gave Mrs. Parsons the jewels. She took them and clasped them around her neck, laughing as she did so.

"And you, I regret to say, Watson," he said, turning to me, "are the unwitting instigator. When you with your great military wisdom pointed out that his fortifications were inadequately guarded, what could a young general do but recruit redcoats wherever he found them?"

I threw up my hands in mock dismay, although in common with everyone there my feelings were of overwhelming relief.

"My friends," said John Parsons, "it is well past noon. Let us go to the dining room and celebrate this joyous day around a table bearing what cook swears is the largest goose in all the Dales."

We cheered our assent and followed him. I offered my right arm to Miss Beck, who slipped her own slim arm through it with a smile. Together we descended the stairs as one of the happiest couples in England that Christmas day.

Also from MX Publishing

MX Publishing is proud to support the campaign to save and restore Sir Arthur Conan Doyle's former home. Undershaw is where he brought Sherlock Holmes back to life, and should be preserved for future generations of Holmes fans.

Save Undershaw   www.saveundershaw.com

Facebook   www.facebook.com/saveundershaw

You can read more about Sir Arthur Conan Doyle and Undershaw in Alistair Duncan's book (share of royalties to the Undershaw Preservation Trust) – An Entirely New Country and in the amazing compilation Sherlock's Home – The Empty House (all royalties to the Trust).

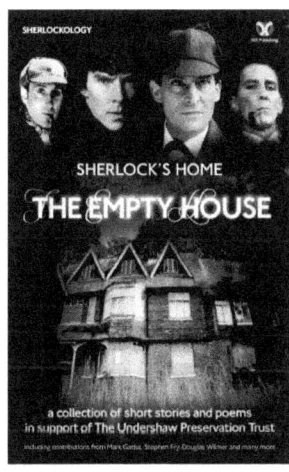

211

Also from MX Publishing

More short story Sherlock Holmes collections

The Oustanding Mysteries of Sherlock Holmes
(Gerard Kelly)

The Untold Adventure of Sherlock Holmes
(Luke Kuhns)

Also from MX Publishing

Sherlock Holmes Travel Guides

In ebook an interactive guide to London

400 locations linked to Google Street View.

Also from MX Publishing

Cross over fiction featuring great villains from history

  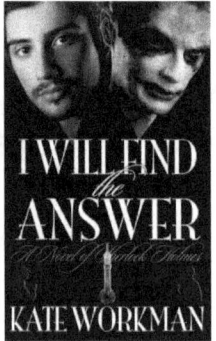

Fantasy Sherlock Holmes

www.mxpublishing.com

Also from MX Publishing

Carrying the seal of the Conan Doyle Estate.....

On the most secret and dangerous assignment of their lives, Sherlock Holmes and Dr. Watson are sent into the newborn Soviet Union to rescue The Romanovs: Nicholas and Alexandra and their innocent children. Will Holmes and Watson be able to change history? Will they even be able to survive?